英語
語音教程

許雪平、付 博 ◎ 主 編

崧燁文化

前 言

在全球化的當今世界，英語語言強大的跨文化交際作用幾乎無可替代。作為語言與思維的有聲載體的英語口語，更是承載著70%以上的信息傳遞任務。當19世紀末的語言研究者們不再甘於落入譯讀古典作品這一無聲語言活動的窠臼，掀起一場教學改革運動的時候，語言教學開始變得有聲有色。語言教學改變了以往2,000多年的規定性語言研究範式，注重詞彙和語法的分析與經典文學著作的翻譯，大膽還原語言的本真，即語言的有聲特質，語音既而成為教學的一個重點內容。此后，儘管語言教學歷經時代變遷，但是語音的根本地位一直不可動搖。

語音受到時間、空間、社會群體以及講話者等諸多因素的影響，存在明顯的語體多樣性，理想的描述性研究不一而足。在中國的教育體制中，從小學、中學到大學，英語教學的重要地位是毋庸置疑的：從小學一年級開設英語課程，直至大學二年級，共14年，平均每週超過4節課。然而當我們對大學非英語專業二年級學生的語音掌握情況進行調查時發現，許多學生不能準確朗讀完整的48個音標符號，多數學生對於英語語音中的失去爆破、連讀、同化、停頓、句子重音、重讀、弱讀、節奏、語調、降調、升調和降升調的基本用法等一無所知或知之甚少。這些調查數據反應出的語音掌握現狀和中國英語教學的氛圍、學生和家長們對其的重視程度是嚴重不成比例的。現有的教學方式並未對學生的語音進行全面、系統的培訓。北京外國語大學的吳冰教授曾說過：「語言是有聲的，因此，一開始就要把語音的基礎打好。只有發音正確，別人才能聽懂你的話，同時也便於你自己通過『聽』來學習新的知識。」語音學習的重要性和中國學生存在的學習問題表明，有必要進行重點音標的糾錯訓練、加強話語節奏感方面的訓練、強化語流音變的概念，克服漢語語音的負遷移影響。

鑒於此，本書剝繭抽絲，尊重權威，以48個國際音標符號為準，在語音的各個方面——語音、語調、重音、音節、重讀、弱讀、輔音連綴、連讀、節奏等，遵照統一的英國BBC語音標準，使用統一的語音術語和符號，標註和解釋各個示例。同時，為拓展學習者的語音知識視野，在音標符號圖解部分，提供了英式、美式和國際音標這三種音標符號。

本書具備科學性、系統性與普適性，兼具理論知識和實踐示例。理論部分深入淺出、通俗易懂，示例內容由簡及繁、形式多樣，從單音、音位組合、詞組、句子、段落乃至篇章，有最小對立對、繞口令，更包括幽默故事等。行文風格科學、客觀，亦不乏樸實、親切之感。另外，針對中國英語學習者的英語語音問題，特別設計了英漢語音對照的內容。

本書既適用於英語專業和非英語專業的語音教學、轉崗教師培訓以及各種培訓班的教學，也可滿足其他英語學習者的語音升級之需，同時也是廣大英語愛好者的語音學習助手。

由於編者水平有限，教程中的紕漏在所難免，敬請廣大讀者、各位同行指正。

編　者

目 錄

第一章　導論 …………………………………………………（1）
　　第一節　國際音標體系 ……………………………………（1）
　　第二節　音素、音標和發音器官 …………………………（3）
　　第三節　英語語音學習的目標 ……………………………（4）
　　第四節　語音學習的問題解疑 ……………………………（9）
　　第五節　朗讀技巧 …………………………………………（12）
第二章　元音 …………………………………………………（15）
　　第一節　單元音（1）：前元音 ……………………………（15）
　　第二節　單元音（2）：中元音 ……………………………（30）
　　第三節　單元音（3）：后元音 ……………………………（43）
　　第四節　雙元音（1）：合口雙元音 ………………………（58）
　　第五節　雙元音（2）：集中雙元音 ………………………（76）
第三章　輔音 …………………………………………………（84）
　　第一節　輔音音標符號及其發音要領 ……………………（84）
　　第二節　輔音字母的發音 …………………………………（89）
第四章　音節 …………………………………………………（98）
　　第一節　音節 ………………………………………………（98）
　　第二節　單詞重音 …………………………………………（101）
第五章　重音和節奏 …………………………………………（105）
第六章　弱讀 …………………………………………………（117）
第七章　輔音連綴 ……………………………………………（125）
　　第一節　輔音連綴 …………………………………………（125）
　　第二節　失去爆破和部分失去爆破 ………………………（128）
第八章　意群 …………………………………………………（134）
第九章　節奏 …………………………………………………（139）
第十章　語調 …………………………………………………（146）
參考文獻 ………………………………………………………（161）
附錄 ……………………………………………………………（163）

第一章 導論

第一節 國際音標體系

一、國際音標 IPA

國際音標（International Phonetic Alphabet），原義是「國際語音字母」，簡稱 IPA，由國際語音協會制定。

1888 年，由英國的 H. 斯維斯特倡議，由法國的 P. 帕西和英國的 D. 瓊斯等人完成，發表在《語音教師》（「國際語音協會」前身「語音教師協會」的會刊）上的 IPA 是歷史上第一個國際音標表。后經多次修訂，現通行的是 2005 年修訂的方案。國際音標嚴格規定以「一符一音」為原則，即「一個音素一個符號，一個符號一個音素」。它以拉丁字母為基礎，但因人類語音差異很大，有限的拉丁字母遠不夠用，於是就用改變字形和借用別的語言的字母的方法來補充。讀音上，為照顧習慣，多數符號仍保留拉丁語或其他語言的原音。

二、DJ 音標

DJ 音標（Daniel Jones Phonetic Symbol，简稱 DJ），作者是英國語言學家 Daniel Jones。

Daniel Jones 根據 IPA 編了一本英國英語的發音辭典 *English Pronouncing Dictionary*，從 1917 年第 1 版推出到 2006 年，共發行了 17 版。他所編的英語發音辭典代表了被稱為「標準讀音」（Received Pronunciation，簡稱 RP）的讀音，這種讀音在受過教育的英國人，尤其是南部英格蘭人中通用。DJ 音標第 14 版的音標符號共計 44 個，其中輔音 24 個，元音 20 個，只包含英式發音。1997 年出版的第 15 版 *English Pronouncing Dictionary* 引入了美式發音。2003 年出版的第 16 版辭典做了很小的改動，增加了新詞並解釋了 150 余個語音術語。2006 年的第 17 版辭典繼續增加了一些新詞並介紹了英語的語音、語調和節奏。

三、KK 音標

KK 音標（Kenyon & Knott Phonetic Symbols，简稱 KK），作者為美國語言學家 John S. Kenyon 和 Thomas A. Knott。

他們編寫的美語發音字典 *Pronouncing Dictionary of American English* 於 1944 年首次出版，裡面所使用的符號均從前面提到的國際音標符號（IPA）而來。

Kenyon 和 Knott 僅將其中適用於美式英語的符號截取出來，再加上美音特有的「兒」音，變成了美式英語的 KK 音標。這是一套最常用的也是最權威的註音法，從此 KK 音標成為代表美語標準發音的音標系統。

四、英文字典裡的單詞讀音

國內的英文字典裡最常見的音標為英式發音的 DJ 音標和美式發音的 KK 音標，前者的根據是 Daniel Jones 編的英語發音字典（*English Pronouncing Dictionary*），后者的根據是 John S. Kenyon 和 Thomas A. Knott 所編的美語發音字典（*A Pronouncing Dictionary of American English*）。值得一提的是，兩種音標所使用的符號均從前面提到的國際音標符號（IPA）而來。

五、英語教材中使用的音標

現今大學英語通用教材之一、「普通高等教育『十一五』國家級規劃教材」——《新視野大學英語》系列教材所採用的音標即為 DJ 音標第 14 版。較早的中學課本通常使用的是 DJ 音標第 13 版，兩者之間的差異使得部分學生接觸大學英語課本時對課本中的音標產生了諸多疑問。表 1-1 是 DJ 音標第 13 版和第 14 版的對比表，相信能解決大家的大部分疑惑。

表 1-1　　　　　DJ 音標第 13 版和第 14 版對比表

音素	分類	DJ 音標第 13 版	DJ 音標第 14 版
元音	單元音	[i:]、[i]、[e]、[æ] [ə:]、[ə]、[ʌ] [u:]、[u]、[ɔ:]、[ɔ]、[ɑ:]	/iː/、/ɪ/、/e/、/æ/ /ɜː/、/ə/、/ʌ/ /uː/、/ʊ/、/ɔː/、/ɒ/、/ɑː/
	雙元音	[ei]、[əu]、[ai]、[au]、[ɔi]、[iə]、[ɛə]、[uə]	/eɪ/、/əʊ/、/aɪ/、/aʊ/、/ɔɪ/、/ɪə/、/eə/、/ʊə/
輔音	爆破音	[p]、[b]、[t]、[d]、[k]、[g]	/p/、/b/、/t/、/d/、/k/、/g/
	摩擦音	[f]、[v]、[θ]、[ð]、[s]、[z]、[ʃ]、[ʒ]、[r]、[h]	/f/、/v/、/θ/、/ð/、/s/、/z/、/ʃ/、/ʒ/、/r/、/h/
	破擦音	[tʃ]、[dʒ]	/tʃ/、/dʒ/
	舌側音	[l]	/l/
	鼻音	[m]、[n]、[ŋ]	/m/、/n/、/ŋ/
	半元音	[w]、[j]	/w/、/j/

值得關注的是，隨著時代的變遷，許多教材、教輔裡的音標體系現在有改成 KK 音標的趨勢。DJ 音標第 15 版也已被廣泛使用。本教程所採用的音標體系為 DJ 音標第 15 版，參照《麥克米倫高階英語辭典（英語版）》。第 15 版與第 14 版

的差別主要體現在/i/、/u/、/x/這三個發音符號上。對於這三種發音出現的情況，將分別在講解元音/ɪ/、/ɒ/和輔音概述的時候詳細描述。

第二節　音素、音標和發音器官

一、音素、音標和發音器官

（一）音素

音素（Phoneme）是根據語音的自然屬性劃分出來的最小語音單位。從聲學性質來看，音素是從音質角度劃分出來的最小語音單位。從生理性質來看，一個發音動作形成一個音素。如：/eg/包含/e/和/g/兩個發音動作，是兩個音素。相同的發音動作形成的音就是同一音素，不同的發音動作發出的音就是不同音素。如/dɒg/和/bæg/中的兩個發音動作相同，是相同音素；/d/和/b/，/ɒ/和/æ/，發音動作不同，是不同音素。對音素的分析，一般是根據發音動作來描寫的。如/m/的發音動作是：上唇和下唇閉攏，聲帶振動，氣流從鼻腔衝出發音，歸類為雙唇鼻音。

（二）音標

音標（Phonetic Symbol）是語音學上用來記錄音素的符號，是音素的標寫符號，如國際音標，一般用「//」標明。它的制定原則是：一個音素只用一個音標表示，一個音標只表示一個音素。如漢語拼音字母、英語的 DJ 音標和美式英語的 KK 音標都是音素的標寫符號。

（三）發音器官

發音動作相同與否決定是否為同一音素，而發音動作的重要構成要件之一為參與發音的部位，即發音器官。為了正確地發音，應該知道發音器官的構成，怎樣運用發音器官發音，怎樣發出的音才準確。

在發音器官中，會活動的發音器官有舌、唇、軟腭、聲帶、牙床。正確地掌握會活動的發音器官的位置和動作，就能發出正確的語音。在發音器官中，舌、唇、牙床在發音時有關聯，例如雙唇收圓並突出時，后舌自然一定會抬高；舌位低時，牙床一定是開的；相反，舌位高時，牙床也必然合攏起來。在學習元音時，舌位很重要，但不易掌握，而唇和牙床的動作容易掌握，可用正確的唇、牙床動作帶出正確的舌位。

圖1-1中標示的即為英語音素發音中的重要發音器官。

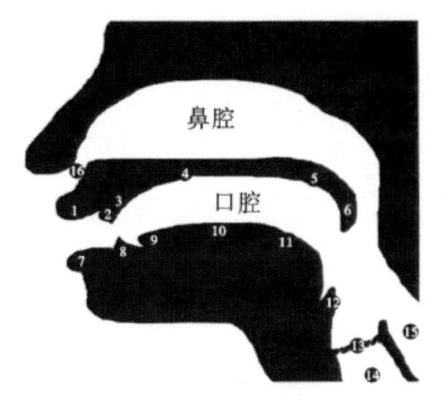

```
1. 上唇
2. 上齒
3. 上齒齦
4. 硬腭
5. 軟腭
6. 小舌
7. 下唇
8. 下齒
9. 舌尖
10. 舌面
11. 舌根
12. 會厭
13. 聲帶
14. 氣管
15. 食道
16. 鼻孔
```

圖 1-1　發音器官圖

二、音素的分類

自從國際語音協會於 1888 年制定了第一套國際音標以來，語音學家們對其進行著不斷地研究和更新。他們普遍認為：根據氣流從肺部呼出時是否受到發音器官的阻礙，語音可以分為元音和輔音兩大類。

（一）元音

在發音時，氣流不受任何發音器官阻礙的音素叫元音。

元音包括：/iː/、/ɪ/、/e/、/æ/、/ɜː/、/ə/、/ʌ/、/uː/、/ʊ/、/ɔː/、/ɒ/、/ɑː/、/eɪ/、/aɪ/、/ɔɪ/、/eʊ/、/aʊ/、/ɪə/、/eə/、/ʊə/ 20 個音素。

（二）輔音

發音時，氣流受到任何一個發音器官阻礙的音素叫輔音。

輔音音素共有 24 個，包括：氣流在雙唇受阻礙的 /p/、/b/、/m/ 和 /w/；氣流在上齒和下唇受阻礙的 /f/ 和 /v/；氣流在舌尖和上齒受阻礙的 /θ/ 和 /ð/；氣流在舌尖和齒齦受阻礙的 /t/、/d/、/s/、/z/、/n/、/l/ 和 /r/；氣流在舌尖和硬腭受阻礙的 /ʃ/、/ʒ/、/tʃ/ 和 /dʒ/；氣流在舌身和硬腭受阻礙的 /j/；氣流在舌后部和軟腭受阻礙的 /k/、/g/ 和 /ŋ/；氣流在喉部受阻礙的 /h/。

第三節　英語語音學習的目標

英語語音學習者如果不瞭解語音學習的理想目標與現實目標之間的區別，其結果便是自尋煩惱。

有一則英文故事這樣說：英國一位老人退休后，決定去倫敦郊外的一個小鎮享受靜謐和諧的田園生活。鎮上人的英語發音幾乎和標準英音相當。老人發現自己的發音很另類，感覺很苦悶：「難道我活了一輩子，連語音都沒學好啊？！垂垂

老年的我哪裡還能學來這樣標準的發音啊！」老人終日悶悶不樂，鬱鬱而終。

　　英語在世界範圍內的廣泛使用，使得其語音呈現多樣性。各種英語語體的語音之間存在著不同程度的差異，如英式英語、美式英語、加拿大英語、澳大利亞英語、愛爾蘭英語、新西蘭英語、新加坡英語、印度英語等，在語音體系和發音方式等方面都有差異。與其他任何語言相類似，英語語音突出的符號性和穩定性特徵使得英語語音的教學和學習具有普遍的規律性和一致性。然而語音學習者在學習目的、學習方式、學習策略等方面的不同，也賦予了語音教學個體差異性。

　　針對不同的英語學習者的不同需求，語音學習的目標應該有所差異。這裡可以採用一個五級量表來區分，即語音很標準、有少許錯誤但不影響交際、有一些錯誤但還不影響交際、有許多錯誤影響交際、錯誤太嚴重無法交際。對於一般的英語愛好者而言，可以容忍其語音有一些錯誤但不影響交際，而對於已經或者即將把英語作為職業的人而言，如教師、口譯員、語音研究者等，英語語音應該很標準。專門從事語音研究的人員，還要瞭解英語語音的地域性特徵，甚至其演變對種族發展的影響。

　　英語語音主要包括以下內容，學習者必須清楚自己的學習目標和學習重點。

· 音標符號（Phonetic Symbols）
· 音節（Syllable）
· 重音（Stress）
· 語調（Intonation）
· 節奏（Rhythm）
· 連讀（Linking）
· 弱讀（Reduction）
· 縮略（Contraction）
· 停頓（Pausing）

　　國家教育部在中小學英語教學這個特殊的領域，針對英語語音學習的階段性和漸進性特徵，在《義務教育英語課程標準》（2011年版）中規定了具體的分級目標。

　　在九級目標體系中，一至五級為義務教育階段的目標要求。其中，一級為起始級別，二級為6年級結束時應達到的基本要求，五級為9年級結束時應達到的基本要求。六至九級為普通高中的目標要求。其中，七級為高中畢業的基本要求，八級和九級是為願意進一步提高英語綜合語言運用能力的高中學生設計的目標。在九個級別的目標中，一級、三級和四級為義務教育階段的過渡級別，六級為高中階段的過渡級別。英語課程分級目標結構如圖1-2所示：

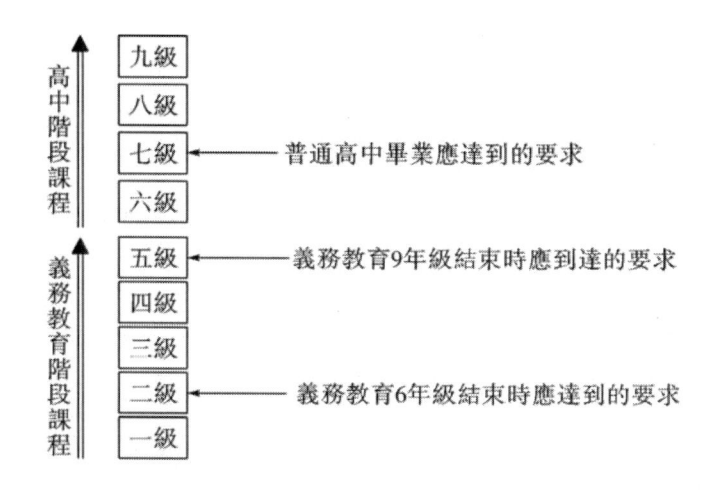

```
高中階段課程  ┌─九級─┐
              │ 八級 │
              │ 七級 │◄── 普通高中畢業應達到的要求
              │ 六級 │
義務教育階段課程┌─五級─┐◄── 義務教育9年級結束時應到達的要求
              │ 四級 │
              │ 三級 │
              │ 二級 │◄── 義務教育6年級結束時應達到的要求
              │ 一級 │
```

圖 1-2　英語課程分級目標結構

一、《義務教育英語課程標準》（2011 年版）關於語音的分級目標

級別	具體目標
二級	1. 正確讀出 26 個英文字母； 2. 瞭解簡單的拼讀規律； 3. 瞭解單詞和句子的重音； 4. 瞭解英語語音包括重音、連讀、語調、節奏、停頓等現象。
五級	1. 瞭解語音在語言學習中的意義； 2. 在日常生活會話中做到語音、語調基本正確、自然、流暢； 3. 根據重音和語調的變化理解和表達不同的意圖和態度； 4. 根據讀音拼寫單詞和短語。
七級	1. 在口頭表述中做到語音、語調自然和流暢； 2. 根據語音、語調瞭解話語中隱含的意圖和態度； 3. 初步瞭解英語詩歌中的節奏和韻律； 4. 根據語音辨別和書寫不太熟悉的單詞。
八級	1. 在交際中逐步做到語音、語調自然、得體和流暢； 2. 根據語音、語調瞭解和表達隱含的意圖和態度； 3. 瞭解詩歌中的節奏和韻律； 4. 根據語音辨別和書寫不太熟悉的單詞或簡單的語句。
九級	1. 在用英語與各國人士進行交談時或在聽不同國家人士講英語的錄音時，能克服不同口音帶來的困難，聽懂大意； 2. 能運用恰當的語調、節奏和重音變化等手段有效地表達不同的語意和態度等交流意圖。

註：六級的教學可參照七級目標要求。

二、英語語音學習的理想目標與現實目標

語音具有突出的物理屬性，從理論上講，語音學習可以達到理想目標。但是，即使是把英語作為職業的中國學習者，對英語語音的目標要求也要做到理想與現實的契合。

(一) 理想目標

英語語音學習的理想目標是發音（國際音標）準確、語流順暢、交際通達，具體指的是音色、音高、音準、連讀、弱讀、節奏、停頓，乃至用語音傳情達意等方面達到至高水平。這類英語學習者期望能夠達到以英語作為本族語者的語音水平。

但是受到諸多因素的制約，在將英語作為外語的中國，英語教學的目標應該更現實一些。

(二) 影響理想目標實現的因素

英語語音學習的理想目標的實現受到普遍性因素和學習者個體因素的制約。

1. 普遍性因素

普遍性因素主要包括生理、性別年齡、語言環境等因素。

生理因素：對語音學習者最基本的要求是生理健全。發音器官包括大腦、神經、口腔、鼻腔、舌頭和牙齒等。這些器官任何一個方面存在缺陷，都會影響基本的發音效果。理想的語音甚至需要學習者擁有健康的體魄。沒有充分的體力和旺盛的精力，語音很可能會音質弱、音色差、缺乏節奏和韻律感，影響交流。

性別年齡因素：就生理性別而言，研究表明，女性的語音器官比男性發育和成熟得更早，因而靈活性更強，在語音學習中呈現出明顯的優勢。

關於人類學習外語的最佳年齡，世界範圍的實證研究結果莫衷一是。有些研究結果認為越早越好，但是有些研究結果表明並非如此。普遍的觀點是外語學習存在一個成熟期，約在 8~11 歲，因人而異。在成熟期之前，語言學習者的大腦和語言神經等的可塑性較強。在此期間學習外語，相對較理想。如果在成熟期之後開始學習外語，則年齡越小，語音學習速度越快，效果越好。相反，年齡越大，語音學習速度越慢，效果越差。

語言環境因素：外語學習受到一個國家語言政策的影響。對於國家推廣的語言，社會對學習者以及學習者自己對於該語言的語音要求也會較高。作為具有強烈社會屬性的外語學習者，不可避免地受到周圍人，尤其是周圍語言環境的影響。語言環境中母語因素越多，語音遷移的可能性就越大，外語語音學習速度和效果越差；反之，周圍環境中目標語言因素越多，母語語音遷移的可能性就會越小，外語學習速度和效果越好。

具有明顯地域屬性的方音對於外語語音學習的影響不可忽視。中國的 56 個

民族，擁有不同的民族方言，甚至在一種方言裡，又有無數種方音。英語語言起源於日耳曼人的盎格魯-薩克森語（Anglo-Saxon），這被稱為「古英語」（Old English, OE），時間大約是5世紀到11世紀。至今歷經16個世紀的發展，語體豐富，語音也是應有盡有。不同語系的語言相似性較小。跨語系的外語學習往往難度比較大。漢語屬於漢藏語系，而英語則屬於印歐語系，英漢語言的元音、韻母的區別很大，加之在中國缺乏足夠的英語語言環境，因此中國的英語學習者學習英語語音的障礙較大。

可見單從語音學習的角度看，積極在國內尋找和創造外語學習環境，甚至到目標語言國家學習和生活是學習理想語音的條件。

2. 個體因素

學習者的個體差異性體現在許多方面，如家庭背景、情感因素、性格因素、認知風格和文化認同等。這些因素都不同程度上影響著中國的英語學習者的發音。

家庭背景：家庭是學生的第一學校。孩子的英語語音學習可以得益於家人的薰陶，也可能受制於家人英語語音知識的缺失或者錯誤。現代中國家庭教育很重要的一個方面就是家長對子女的英語學習的影響。目前一些中小學英語教材中設置的課外活動，就是要求學生和家長進行英語口語互動的項目。

情感因素：中國學習者對英語語音的學習動機、興趣、信心、意志以及與他人合作的精神等都會影響到其英語語音的學習。

中國的英語學習者應首先充分認識到英語在人類交融、國家發展和個人發展等方面的巨大意義，瞭解英語學習的工具性和人文性雙重屬性，從而產生強烈的外在與內在動機，努力發現和體會英語語音的魅力和多重功能，保持學習的興趣。同時，由於英語語音與漢語語音之間存在的較大差異，學習者不免會遇到許多問題，有些障礙甚至很難克服，這就需要學習者要有百折不撓、迎難而上的堅強意志和必勝的信心。維果斯基的最近發展區理論指出，學習者在學習過程中最受益於與自己最近的共同學習者。要提高自己的語音水平，學習者就要主動建立和融入語音學習的共同體，善於發現問題，主動求教，主動幫助他人，精於合作，樂於分享，才能不斷提高自己的語音水平。

性格因素：一般情況下，外向型性格的學習者，敢於和樂於實踐和嘗試不同的事物，所以在英語語音學習方面會較主動地接受和練習。內向型性格的人，則願意自己默讀英語，在利用最近發展區進行學習方面，羞於在同伴面前嘗試，不善表達，從而影響其英語語音的學習。家長和教師應該引導這些學習者，幫助他們變得開朗，在英語語音學習方面大膽嘗試。

認知風格：英語語音的學習也會受到學習者認知風格的影響。場依賴者難以擺脫母語或其他已學外語語音的影響。某些大學英語專業的學生甚至在碩士研究生階段由於受到漢語的影響，還不能對英語重音產生語感。與此類學習者形成對

照的是，場獨立者則可以較快地獲得對英語的語感，擺脫漢語語音的干擾。

文化認同：語言是文化的載體。語音學習受到學習者文化認同程度的影響。一般來說，對英語文化感興趣或者抱有積極肯定態度的英語學習者，在英語語音學習方面會較主動地傾注精力和時間，自覺地模仿地道的語音。

(三) 現實目標

在中國，英語是被作為外語來學的，沒有足夠的語言環境，即使具備了其他條件，理想的英語語音目標也不可能實現。英語學習者應該明白這個道理，不可妄自菲薄。制定理性、現實的語音學習目標，才能為學好英語語音指明方向。

自然流暢（Smooth）：英語語音的標準自19世紀80年代以來一直採用「國際語音學會」規定的「標準音標」，之後的多次修訂確保了這套符號不朽的生命力。雖然有些學者，包括中國的趙元任教授等，曾經和正在倡導自然語音，但是這種主張一時還很難得到全世界把英語作為外語的國家的廣泛認同。

由於上述諸多因素的影響，精確的標準英語語音對於絕大多數中國的英語學習者來說不可企及，但是可以做到英語語音自然流暢，形成語流。

可理解（Intelligible）：語音的首要和基本的達意功能要求學習者的英語語音要讓將英語作為本族語者聽得懂。過於不正確的語音會讓人費解。許多中國的英語學習者忽視英語中的單詞重音的作用，從而導致交際受阻的案例不勝枚舉。

交際有效（Effective in Communication）：英語語音在交際中的作用不僅體現在音準、流暢等方面，還體現在對交際質量的保障作用上。當交際的內容不成問題時，良好的交際質量就要求語音要傳情、傳神，這是對英語語音學習的高層次要求。避免學習者拿腔作勢，用自認為或想像中的語音講英語。

在英語課堂上，教師應該從學生英語學習的初始階段，就通過歌曲、音視頻故事、小短劇等培養學生對英語語音在傳情達意方面作用的意識。隨後要在全學段培養學生重視英語語音在有效、高質交際方面的作用，提高其英語語音的鑒賞能力和品位。

第四節　語音學習的問題解疑

一、什麼是好的語音？

對於我們中國人學英語，語音的最高標準當然是能和英語國家的人說得一樣或基本上接近。然而，這樣的要求是很高的，達到這種要求也是很困難的。實際上需要語音十分標準的人只是少數，如以中文為母語的英語播音員、專業英語教師等。對於我們大多數人來說，能做到以下幾點就應該算是擁有好的語音：

元音、輔音音素基本正確，發音清晰；

語調（包括升調和降調）基本正確；

語速適中；
語流沒有太多斷句和停頓；
交際時對方聽得明白，不需要請你多次重複；
會話基本能自然順利地進行。

二、我能學好語音嗎？

大多數人都能學好語音，但首先要解決一個認識問題。影響我們學好語音的因素有許多，如：

口音（對中國人來說即是中國口音或各地方的口音）；
年齡（年齡越小越容易接受新的語音）；
個人受英語環境熏陶時間的長短；
聽覺感官能力的差異；
先天和個性的差異；
個人學習態度和學習動力的差異等。

以上絕大多數差異都是可以通過接受正規訓練，通過自身的努力和不斷調整自己的心態和認識等方式得到改善並加以糾正的。

三、我怎樣學習語音呢？

（1）學習英語語音就像學習藝術一樣。像練鋼琴、習字繪畫、跳芭蕾一樣，「練」是核心，是關鍵。要天天練，時時練，不間斷地練。不能操之過急，要懂得循序漸進的道理。

（2）在正確的指導下練。要有正確的、正規的語音指導，如：直接接受教師指導，用聽錄音、聽廣播等方式來學語音。這樣你就可以打好基礎，練好基本功。就像學鋼琴一樣，有了正確的指法指導訓練，還要通過刻苦的練習，才能最終學好語音。

（3）學習語音要抱著「從頭學」的態度。「從頭學」的意思是把英語語音作為一種全新的事物去學，不要去找「捷徑」——從漢語中去找「相同」的音來替代英語中的音。可以這樣說，英語音素中有和漢語拼音相似的音，如/iː/、/ɑː/、/m/等，但沒有完全相同的音。這樣的替代只是滿足你初學語音時的需要，長遠來說很可能貽誤時機，造成終身的遺憾。因為一旦形成了錯誤的發音，要想糾正，需要花上雙倍甚至更多的時間和努力。

（4）練習語音越早效果越好，越早練越容易糾正錯誤，越早練越可以贏得時間。但是，一句英語成語說得好：「Never too late to learn.」（學習永遠不會太晚，任何時候開始學習都來得及。）千里之行，始於足下，請你今天就開始吧！

四、我是學英國音還是學美國音？

就語音而言，英國音和美國音在少數元音和輔音上有些差別，如元音/ʌ/，

/ɔ/，輔音/r/等。英音和美音的語調也有些差異。但是，就語音的基本功來說，英音和美音是一樣的。英國音和美國音在發音上的差別不會影響交際時相互之間的理解，正如我們漢語中普通話和香港、臺灣地區的普通話雖然在語音上有些差異，但並不影響互相交流一樣。因此不論你想學英國音還是學美國音，練好基本功，找準英語語音的感覺才是最重要的。

五、音標為什麼有時用方括弧（[　]）有時用斜線（/　/）？

/　/和[　]都是音標符號。但是，/　/和[　]所標出的音素在概念和意義上是不同的。

/　/：音位音標，是一種寬式音標。這種音標用一個符號標示一個音位。音位是最小的能區分意義的單位，更適用於一般語言教學。

[　]：語音音標，是一種嚴式音標。這種音標可以用幾種符號來描述一個音，更多為專業語音研究人員使用。

嚴式音標符號繁多，非常難記，如[ε]，[œ]等。至此，我們已經明白，對於我們一般人學外語，音位音標更接近我們的需要。在學習 tenth 這個詞的時候，無疑多數人是會選擇/tenθ/的。

相信以上說明可以解答這本書中為什麼要用斜線/　/來表示音標這個問題了。（應該指出的是，目前很多仍用[　]來表示音位的現象是需要糾正的。）

六、什麼是學語音的「靈丹妙藥」？

應該說學語音是沒有靈丹妙藥的，也是沒有捷徑的。不過，學習語音是有好方法的，有時還會有竅門。最好的方法就是聽和模仿。

聽：可以提高你的辨音能力。要聽正確的語音，聽教師的示範，聽好的錄音帶。要努力把自己置身在一個英語的環境中。只要你用心聽，久而久之就會受到英語美妙動聽的音調的熏陶。聽，不但會給你帶來享受，還會使你有一個高標準和目標，不斷地激勵你去追求和攀登。

模仿：不聽，光自己讀，是學習語音的誤區。光聽不模仿，則是學習語音的另一個誤區。要大膽地模仿，大聲地讀和說，要背誦詩歌和短文。希望這本書給大家提供的詩歌和短文能成為你們學好語音的良師益友。只要你持之以恒，就會有明顯的進步。

把英語語音完全當作一種新的知識和技能來學，從頭學。不要借助漢語拼音或其他外語。這樣反而會事倍功半。一旦形成錯誤的語音，就要花上雙倍甚至幾倍的時間去糾正。「從頭學」才是最好的辦法，因為在一張白紙上才能畫出最新、最美的圖畫。

第五節　朗讀技巧

　　清晨的校園，常常可以看到一些學生在朗讀英語。他們中間有一些人讀得悅耳動聽，還有一些人雖然十分努力，卻讀得錯誤百出。讀錯的原因有兩個：一是因為缺乏教師的指導而無法掌握朗讀技巧，二是對語音語流的細微變化不善於分辨和琢磨思考。學習並不一定是花的時間越多效果就越好。如果方法不得當，雖然花了很多時間卻難以收到預期的效果，有時還會適得其反。英語朗讀是幫助學生復習和記憶所學知識的一種好方法，它更可以使人體會和享受語言給人帶來的美感，應該大力提倡。下面談一談提高英語朗讀水平應該注意的幾個主要方面。

一、提高朗讀，聽力先行

　　英語不是我們的母語，它的語音語調是我們所不能創造的。一個人需要學習相當一段時間才能夠比較自如地運用正確的語音語調進行朗讀和交流。語音語調必須通過模仿才能學會。模仿的前提是聽。只有聽得準，才能學得像。有些學生見文章就讀，從不或很少認真模仿他人的讀法，當然就讀不好。

　　開始練習朗讀，應該在教師的具體指導下從有錄音的段落或章節練起，要選擇發音準確、難易適度、讀速較慢的錄音。太難的錄音會將練習者的注意力引到詞義上去。內容簡單可以省去很多花在生詞上的時間。讀速較慢的錄音有利於學習者聽清每一個詞的確切發音、詞與詞之間的連接與音調，便於進行逐字逐句的模仿。詞句讀得準確，才能為段落朗讀打下堅實的基礎。待慢速朗讀收到成效之后，再換聽讀速較快的錄音。

　　模仿的錄音內容以短為宜。語言如同音樂，吐字與音調升降過程中有許多細小的修飾，並不是一兩遍就可以聽得出、學得會的，必須反覆加深印象。聽得越多、品味越細、理解越深，才能學得越像。章節太長，聽一遍就要很長時間，容易使人疲乏厭倦，無法對所有的細微變化產生深刻的印象。錄音短小而精悍，便於學習者重複聽，仔細體會他人的發聲或朗讀技巧。聽音時注意力要集中。一些學生聽音時易打瞌睡，說明用心不夠。還有的人在睡覺前聽音，這種方法聽新聞尚可，模仿發音則不可取，應當予以糾正。

二、用心模仿，不厭其煩

　　多聽的目的是為了模仿，而模仿是一種需要反覆進行、非常枯燥卻又十分必要的實踐活動，不能有任何厭煩情緒。運動員在比賽場上每一次有效的衝擊，都需要有平時每一個動作千百次苦練的基礎。鄧亞萍不會因為打了一個好球就認為自己可以得冠軍。即使當了冠軍，如果想保持好的成績，她依然每天要練習那些最基本的動作。宋祖英不會因為唱好了一首歌便認為自己可以當歌唱家。雖然她

已經成名，但如果想久站舞臺，也必須像音樂學院的學生一樣每天練嗓子。學英語的人不能因為發對了某個音就從此不再練習。中國人民解放軍少將、南京通信工程學院原副院長鐘道隆教授45歲開始自學英語，后成為著名的英語翻譯。他聽壞了9臺錄音機、3臺收音機、4臺單放機，翻爛了兩本英語辭典。20歲左右的年輕人只要有他一半的勤奮，就能學好英語。

模仿時除了要注意音和調以外，還要特別注意連讀和失去爆破。在語言實踐中，有許多單詞由於受到前后單詞的影響而在發音的位置、輕重、寬窄、長短方面有所變化。連讀和失去爆破是比較典型的現象。有的同學單音、單詞都發得很準確，連成句子時發音就顯得生硬。原因就在於不懂得單詞發音在句子中有時會發生變化，連讀和失去爆破掌握得不好。

除了連讀和失去爆破，還要特別注意句子重音和說話人的感情。同一個句子，感情不同，讀法也不同。不注意感情特點，會造成朗讀平淡，或因句子重音錯誤而造成不必要的誤解。

模仿的效果如何，取決於能否隨時發現自己的朗讀與示範朗讀之間的差別。只要勤奮用心，這一點並不難做到。怕的是讀錯了，老師也糾正了，但卻不做任何標記，更談不上日后練習，這樣是很難進步的。

三、掌握讀速，循序漸進

練習朗讀時速度不宜太快，初練時尤以慢速清晰為好。

一些老師常常會在課堂上讓學生朗讀課文。很多學生常常讀得很快，以示自己很熟練，但實際上讀錯的地方很多，效果並不理想。這裡有兩個誤區需要指出。

第一，很多人認為讀得快或者說得快就說明英語好，這種看法並不完全正確。一個人英語的好壞並不是用語速來衡量的。中央電視臺某一屆《希望之星》英語大賽中有一位選手各方面都表現得很出色，很有希望拿冠軍。但她說話時的語速太快，一位外國評委說她像一挺機關槍，聽眾沒有時間反應她都說了些什麼。結果本應得冠軍的她僅得了亞軍。其實，外國人平時說話的速度並不快，甚至很慢。他們只有在激動、生氣或者著急的時候說話才會快。新聞記者說話很快，因為他們要在最短的時間裡報導最多的消息。

第二，人都是有表現欲的，想顯示一下自己的水平，這可以理解。但這種表現必須有紮實、熟練的基本功來支撐。當你還沒有掌握本章前幾節中所講的最基本的語音技巧時，先不要急於讀得太快，而應該首先做到讀得清晰、準確。

英語句子中的輕重音節構成許多不同模式的節奏，這些重音和節奏對於劃分意群和句子意思的表達都非常重要（見「節奏」和「意群」部分）。讀速過快會造成句子重音、意群和節奏方面的錯誤，還會造成發音不到位、加音、吞音、誤讀以及移行時的突然中斷，影響意思的表達。

當然，朗讀速度也不是越慢越好。隨著熟練程度的加深和技巧的提高，讀速可以逐步加快，以中速為好。

四、眼口配合，從容流暢

若要朗讀流暢，必須使眼睛在閱讀時保持一定的提前量。戰士打固定的靶子，只要瞄準就可以了。打活靶則不同，必須依照靶子移動的速度和方向來確定瞄準時的提前量。速度越快，提前量越多。朗讀也是一樣。單詞很短，如同一個點，「瞄」起來很容易，讀起來也不難。句子就不同，它如同一條線，朗讀時不容許隨意中斷。要想做到詞與詞之間快慢銜接恰到好處，就不能看一個詞，讀一個詞，而必須使眼睛在閱讀時始終保持一個提前量。提前量的多少根據朗讀速度而定。讀速越快，提前量越多。句子中的標點符號和意群停頓時的間隙都為提前閱讀做好了鋪墊。

英語朗讀不僅反應學生的語音掌握情況，它還反應學生的詞彙量和理解能力。詞彙量少，理解能力差，朗讀中就會有許多障礙。因此，朗讀水平的提高除了需要掌握上述技巧外，還要注意全面提高英語水平。

龐中華老師在他的《龐中華鋼筆字帖》中有這樣一段話，「許多青少年朋友會問：我每天應該寫多少字？我一天寫得不少，為什麼效果不明顯呢？這使我們想起『小猴摘玉米』的故事……我們學寫字的時候，如果每天選一千個不同的字，每個字寫一遍，那麼，很可能一個字也記不牢、寫不好，就像小猴把玉米全丟掉一樣。我們可以改進一下方法：每天選三到五個字，每個字認真多練幾遍，雖然寫字的總數少得多，但練習的效果卻好得多。」

希望大家練習朗讀時能夠做到少而精。

第 二 章 元音

　　發元音時，氣流從肺中壓出，經過氣管進入口腔，在口腔中受到發音器官如舌、唇等的調節，但不受阻礙。舌的前後、高低，唇的圓扁，都會影響從肺中流出的氣流，使之發出不同的元音來。元音發音時聲帶振動。

　　英語共有 20 個元音，依據音的構成，分成由一個音組成的單元音，共 12 個，和由兩個音合二為一的雙元音，共 8 個。

　　單元音的發音共性有：①沒有舌位的移動；②發音過程中，氣流不受任何發音器官的阻礙；③發音過程中沒有任何摩擦。

　　雙元音的發音共性有：①有舌位的移動，過渡自然連貫；②發音過程中，氣流不受任何發音器官的阻礙；③由第一個音向第二個音滑動時，第一個音飽滿、響亮。第二個音短、弱、含糊。

　　根據發音時舌活動的範圍，英語單元音可分為前元音（/iː/、/ɪ/、/e/、/æ/）、中元音（/ɜː/、/ə/、/ʌ/）和后元音（/uː/、/ʊ/、/ɔː/、/ɒ/、/ɑː/）。

　　如圖 2-1 所示，根據發音時舌的滑動方向，英語雙元音可分成合口雙元音（/eɪ/、/aɪ/、/ɔɪ/、/əʊ/、/aʊ/）和集中雙元音（/ɪə/、/eə/、/ʊə/）。

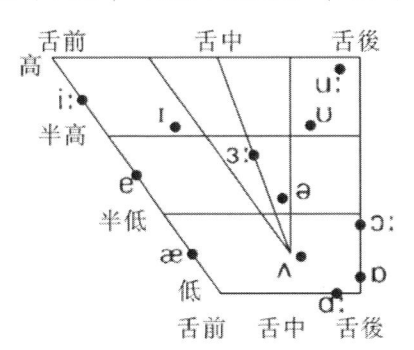

圖 2-1　合口雙元音與集中雙元音舌位圖

第一節　單元音（1）：前元音

　　英語前元音的發音有如下共同特徵：①舌端靠近下齒；②舌前部向上齒齦抬起，但不接觸；③氣流未受到任何阻礙，沒有任何摩擦。

　　英語前元音的發音有如下漸變特徵：① /iː/、/ɪ/、/e/、/æ/的舌位由高到低；② /iː/、/ɪ/、/e/、/æ/的開口程度由小到大。

一、/iː/

（一）/iː/的發音要領
/iː/的發音要領如圖 2-2 所示：

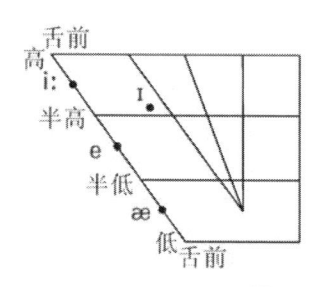

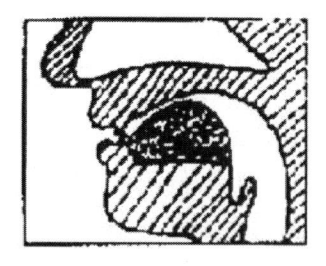

圖 2-2　前元音/iː/

發音部位：舌尖抵下齒。
舌位：舌前部向硬腭抬起，是四個前元音中最高的。
口型：開合度小，成扁平狀。
綜述：/iː/是長元音、前元音。發音時舌尖抵下齒；舌前部向硬腭抬起，舌位較高，是四個前元音中舌位最高的。發音時，雙唇向兩旁平伸成扁平形，口腔肌肉較緊張。

（二）/iː/的發音組合
1. 字母組合 ee 常常讀為前元音/iː/。
breeze　　creep　　deed　　eel　　feet
greet　　jeep　　keen　　meet　　speech
2. 字母組合 ea 常常讀為前元音/iː/。
bean　　cheat　　dean　　eat　　heat　　lean
mean　　neat　　pea　　read　　seat　　weak
3. 字母 e 在重讀音節中常常讀為前元音/iː/。
eve　　even　　evening　　me
she　　Peter　　these　　he
4. 字母組合 ei 常常讀作/iː/。
deceive　　perceive　　receive
5. 字母組合 ie 常常讀為前元音/iː/。
thief　　brief　　relief
believe　　field　　relieve
6. 字母 i 偶爾讀為前元音/iː/。
police
7. 字母組合 eo 偶爾讀為前元音/iː/。
people

8. 字母組合 ey 偶爾讀為前元音 /iː/。
key

(三) /iː/ 的常見發音錯誤辨析

常見錯誤：
(1) 母語化：中國學生容易把元音 /iː/ 讀成漢語中的「衣」音。
(2) 他音化：發音過於接近短元音 /ɪ/。

原因辨析：
(1) 舌身太高，與上顎發生了摩擦。
(2) 舌身太低，口腔肌肉過於放松。

(四) /iː/ 的發音練習

1. 單詞朗讀：

詞首	
eat /iːt/ 吃	each /iːtʃ/ 每一個
east /iːst/ 東邊	ease /iːz/ 容易
easy /ˈiːzɪ/ 容易的	eagle /ˈiːgl/ 鷹
ego /ˈiːgəʊ/ 自我	even /ˈiːvən/ 甚至
equal /ˈiːkwəl/ 平等的	evening /ˈiːvnɪŋ/ 晚上
詞中	
deep /diːp/ 深的	keep /kiːp/ 保持
jeep /dʒiːp/ 吉普車	feed /fiːd/ 喂養
seed /siːd/ 種子	sheep /ʃiːp/ 綿羊
dream /driːm/ 夢	team /tiːm/ 隊
meat /miːt/ 肉	seat /siːt/ 座位
詞尾	
fee /fiː/ 費用	key /kiː/ 答案
she /ʃiː, ʃɪ/ 她	see /siː/ 看見
tea /tiː/ 茶	we /wiː, wɪ/ 我們
free /friː/ 自由的	tree /triː/ 樹
agree /əˈgriː/ 同意	degree /dɪˈgriː/ 程度

2. 短語朗讀：

eat a lot of meat 吃很多肉	feel very weak 感到身體虛弱
green leaves 綠葉子	in the deep sea 在深海中
in three weeks 在三周內	keep it secret 保守秘密
leave the team 離開隊伍	meet in the street 在街頭相遇
see no reason 沒有理由	sweet dreams 甜蜜的夢

3. 句子朗讀：

Seeing is believing.
眼見為實。
There are three trees along the street.
沿街有三棵樹。
A friend in need is a friend indeed.
共患難的朋友才是真正的朋友。
The delegation is leaving Beijing next week.
代表團將於下周離開北京。

(五) 欣賞

1. 童謠：

See the breeze teasing the tree,
Weaving the leaves or shaking them free,
Tossing the fleece of sheep, that keep
On peacefully feeding, half asleep.

2. 歌曲片段：

TAKE ME HOME, COUNTRY ROAD
Almost heaven, West Virginia
Blue Ridge Mountains, Shenandoah River
Life is old there, older than the trees
Younger than the mountains, blowing like a breeze.

LEMON TREE
When I was just a lad of ten
My father said to me
Come here and take a lesson from the lovely lemon tree.
「Don't put your faith in love, my boy,」my father said to me.
「I fear you'll find that love is like the lovely lemon tree.」
(Chorus) Lemon tree, very pretty, and the lemon flower is sweet.
But the fruit of the poor lemon is impossible to eat.
Lemon tree, very pretty, and the lemon flower is sweet.
But the fruit of the poor lemon is impossible to eat.

二、/ɪ/

（一）/ɪ/的發音要領

/ɪ/的發音要領如圖 2-3 所示：

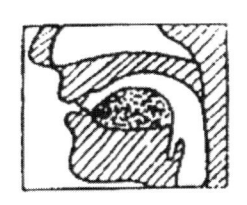

圖 2-3　前元音/ɪ/

發音部位：舌前部須向硬腭抬起。
舌位：比/i:/稍低，稍后。
口型：扁平，開口比/i:/稍大，接近半閉，下顎稍下垂，舌前部也比發/i:/時稍下降。
綜述：/ɪ/是短元音、前元音。發音時舌尖抵下齒；舌前部稍抬起，舌位比/i:/低，扁平唇型。

（二）/ɪ/的發音組合

1. 字母 i 常常讀為前元音/ɪ/。
it　　　　　is　　　　　this　　　　　in　　　　　with
middle　　kitchen　　bridge　　give　　interested
2. 字母 e 常常讀為前元音/ɪ/，尤其在非重讀音節中。
economy　　effect　　elect　　England　　English
equality　　equipment　　erect　　escape　　pretty
3. 字母 a 在 ge 前面的非重讀音節中常常為前元音/ɪ/。
courage　　manage　　message　　voyage　　luggage
damage　　village　　shortage　　language　　advantage
4. 字母 o 的讀音偶爾讀為前元音/ɪ/。
women
5. 字母組合 ui 偶爾讀為前元音/ɪ/。
building

（三）/ɪ/的常見發音錯誤辨析

常見錯誤：
（1）母語化：很多學生常把元音/ɪ/讀成漢語中的「一」。
（2）他音化：中國學生常把短元音/ɪ/發成像長元音/i:/。
（3）他音化：中國學生常把/ɪ/發成像/e/。
（4）單元音雙元音化：把/ɪ/發成像/eɪ/等雙元音。

原因辨析：

（1）舌前部抬得太高，接觸了上顎，發生了摩擦。

（2）口腔肌肉不要繃得太緊，要放鬆，舌面位置要稍降低，不要抬得過於貼近上顎，嘴唇開口要略大。

（3）舌前部位置要稍抬高些，嘴唇開口略收緊。

（4）發音過程中口型有滑動；整個發音過程中，口型應保持在固定位置。

註：在 DJ 第 15 版音標中，增加了 /i/ 這個符號，原因是：在當今的英國英語和美國英語中，常會發現 /ɪ/ 和 /iː/ 這兩個音的界限變得模糊了。例如：city 和 seedy 的結尾元音既不是 /ɪ/，也不是 /iː/。鑒於此，遇到這種情況，用 /i/ 這個符號。現在總結一下 /i/ 這個音通常出現的幾種情況：

（1） /ɪ/ 通常不出現在詞尾。在詞尾的合口元音，如果是非重讀，用 /i/ 來標。如：pretty/ˈprɪti/ 等。

（2）在像 busybody 這樣的複合詞中，/i/ 可以允許在詞中出現。busybody 標為 /ˈbɪzɪbɒdi/。

（3）在非重讀音節中，/ɪ/ 音如果出現在另一個元音之前，用 /i/ 來標。如：curious/ˈkjʊəriəs/，scurry/ˈskʌri/ 等。

（四） /ɪ/ 的發音練習

1. 單詞朗讀：

詞首	
is/ɪz, z, s/ 是	it/ɪt/ 它
ill/ɪl/ 生病的	ink/ɪŋk/ 墨水
idiom/ˈɪdɪəm/ 成語	idiot/ˈɪdɪət/ 白痴
issue/ˈɪsjuː/ 問題	imply/ɪmˈplaɪ/ 暗示
invest/ɪnˈvest/ 投資	ignore/ɪgˈnɔː/ 忽視
詞中	
big/bɪg/ 大的	city/ˈsɪti/ 城市
limit/ˈlɪmɪt/ 限制	little/ˈlɪtl/ 小的
live/lɪv/ 生活	minister/ˈmɪnɪstə/ 部長
rich/rɪtʃ/ 富有的	sister/ˈsɪstə/ 姐妹
ticket/ˈtɪkɪt/ 累	visit/ˈvɪzɪt/ 拜訪

2. 短語朗讀：

visit a big city 去大城市	his little sister 他的小妹
at the ticket office 在售票處	this district 在這個區
zip your lips 閉嘴	daily activities 日常活動
see a film 看電影	go swimming 去遊泳
go fishing 去釣魚	go for a picnic 去野餐
go to an exhibition 去看展覽	finish a report 寫完報告

3. 句子朗讀：

He still stays with us.
他還和我們在一起。
Lily lives in a very big city.
莉莉住在一座大城市裡。
There are sixty-six kids in this district.
這個區有 66 個小孩。
It makes me sick to think of my silly mistake.
想到我犯的愚蠢錯誤我就不舒服。
Kitty's little sister studies American history in Mississippi University.
基蒂的小妹在密西西比大學學美國歷史。

（五）欣賞

1. 繞口令：

It's a pity it's still misty in this city of Italy.
If I assist a sister-assistant, will the sister's sister-assistant assist me?

The lady expecting a baby is looking at the lady with a baby and is
thinking of something about her own future baby.

I wish to wish the wish you wish to wish, but if you wish the wish
the witch wishes, I won't wish the wish you wish to wish.

2. 對話：

Tony： Hi, Mary!
Mary： Hi, Tony!
Tony： Who is this lady?
Mary： Which lady?
Tony： The lady with a baby.
Mary： Oh, she is Kim from Mississippi. She is a typist in a company.
Tony： Mississippi? Is it a big city?
Mary： No, it is not a city. It's a state in America.

3. 童謠：

Silly Billy! Silly Billy!
Why is Billy silly?
Silly Billy hid a shilling,
Isn't Billy Silly?

「Tick」the clock says,「tick, tick, tick」
What you have to do, do quick;
Time is gliding fast away.
For motherland let us do our bit.

The fish in the river swiftly swim,
And slip through the weeds with a silver gleam.
Till they flick their fins and rise with a swish,
To nibble the midges that skim the stream.

4. 歌曲:

ONE LITTLE INDIAN BOY

One little, two little, three little Indians;
Four little, five little, six little Indians;
Seven little, eight little, nine little Indians;
Ten little Indian boys.
Ten little, nine little, eight little Indians;
Seven little, six little, five little Indians;
Four little, three little, two little Indians;
One little Indian boy.

QUE SERA SERA

When I was just a little girl,
I asked my mother,「What will I be?
Will I be pretty? Will I be rich?」
Here's what she said to me,
(Chorus)
「Que sera, sera,
Whatever will be, will be.
The future's not ours to see.
Que sera, sera,
What will be, will be.」
When I grew up and fell in love
I asked my sweetheart,「What lies ahead?
Will we have rainbows day after day?」
Here's what my sweetheart said.
(Chorus)
Now I have children of my own
They ask their mother,「What will I be?
Will I be handsome? Will I be rich?」
I tell them tenderly.
(Chorus)

註: Que sera sera 意為:「該怎樣就怎樣」, 西班牙語, 和英語 whatever will be, will be 同義。

三、/e/

(一) /e/的發音要領

/e/的發音要領如圖 2-4 所示：

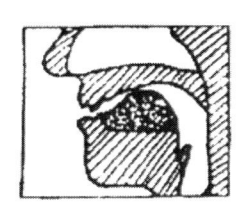

圖 2-4　前元音/e/

發音部位：舌尖抵下齒。
舌位：舌前部向硬腭抬起的高度介於/ɪ/和/æ/之間。
口型：牙床介於半開半合之間，比/ɪ/的牙床略大，雙唇向兩邊張開呈扁平形，呈微笑狀。
綜述：/e/是短元音、前元音。發音時舌尖抵下齒；舌前部稍抬起，高度介於/ɪ/和/æ/之間，扁平唇型。音短、有力。

(二) /e/的發音組合

1. 字母 e 在重讀閉音節中的讀音常常為前元音/e/。

met   well   yet   very   hotel
lecture   pencil   spend   tennis   welcome

2. 字母組合 ea 的讀音常常為前元音/e/。

bread   dead   head   meant   ready
already   measure   peasant   pleasure   weather

3. 字母組合 ai 的讀音常常為前元音/e/。

again   said

4. 字母 a 在重讀閉音節中的讀音常常為前元音/e/。

any   many

5. 字母組合 ay 的讀音偶爾讀為前元音/e/。

says

(三) /e/的常見發音錯誤辨析

常見錯誤：
(1) 他音化：中國學生在讀/e/音時，發音類似/æ/。
(2) 單元音雙元音化：把/e/發成類似/eɪ/的雙元音。
原因辨析：
(1) 舌位抬得太高，需要把舌位壓低些；開口過大，正確的口形是介於半

合和半開之間，接近半合。

（2）發音過程中口型有滑動；整個發音過程中，口型應保持在固定位置。

（四）/e/的發音練習

1. 單詞朗讀：

詞首
end/end/結局　　　　　　　　　　egg/eg/雞蛋
envy/ˈenvɪ/妒忌　　　　　　　　　edit/ˈedɪt/編輯
empty/ˈemptɪ/空的　　　　　　　　elephant/ˈelɪfənt/大象
anyone/ˈenɪwʌn/任何人　　　　　　anything/ˈenɪθɪŋ/任何事
anywhere/ˈenɪweə/任何地方　　　　everything/ˈevrɪθɪŋ/每件事
詞中
bed/bed/床　　　　　　　　　　　forget/fəˈget/忘記
let/let/讓　　　　　　　　　　　　letter/ˈletə/信件
mend/mend/修補　　　　　　　　　never/ˈnevə/從不
red/red/紅色的　　　　　　　　　　rest/rest/休息
step/step/腳步　　　　　　　　　　tent/tent/帳篷

2. 短語朗讀：

my best pen friend 我最好的筆友　　　　　welcome the guests 歡迎客人
refresh my memory 使我重新想起　　　　　set up a restaurant 開個飯館
remember them forever 永遠記住他們　　　the next century 下個世紀
take effective measures 採取有效措施　　　step by step 一步步地
get ready for the wedding 為婚禮做好準備
a fellow she met at a film festival 她在電影節上遇到的一個小伙子

3. 句子朗讀：

Better late than never.
遲做總比不做好。
All is well that ends well.
結局好一切都好。
East or west, home is best.
金窩銀窩不如自家的草窩。／天涯無處似家鄉。
Let's get together when the weather is better.
讓我們在天氣好轉后聚一聚。
I will never forget the splendid time we spent together.
我永遠不會忘記我們一起度過的美好時光。

(五) 欣賞

1. 繞口令：

He sent ten men to mend the dent in the engines of the tender.
Ted sent Fred ten hens yesterday, so Fred's fresh bread is ready already.
Ten wealthy men met twelve beggars and fed them with fresh eggs and bread.

(2) 童謠：

Good, better, best, Never let it rest, Till good is better, And better best.
To tell that Ted is well, That Ben and Bess are better, And that Ned says he is best of all, Let's send a special letter.

四、/æ/

(一) /æ/的發音要領

/æ/的發音要領如圖 2-5 所示：

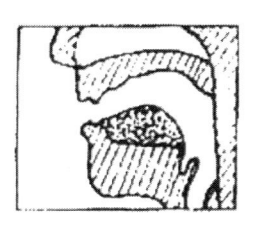

圖 2-5　前元音/æ/

發音部位：舌尖抵下齒。

舌位：舌前部稍抬高，是四個前元音中最低的。

口型：開合度較大，是四個前元音中開口最大的，約兩指寬。

綜述：/æ/是短元音、前元音。發音時舌尖抵下齒；舌前部稍抬起，舌位較低，扁平唇型，上下齒間兩指寬的間距。音短、急促、有力。

(二) /æ/的發音組合

字母 a 在重讀閉音節中的讀音常常為前元音/æ/。

| am | bag | dad | hand | thank |
| campus | factory | family | graduate | blackboard |

（三）/æ/的常見發音錯誤辨析

常見錯誤：

（1）圓唇扁唇化：bag —/beg/；cat —/ket/

（2）單元音雙元音化：back—/baɪk/；black —/blaɪk/

（3）母語化：讀成中文的「哀」或「愛」，如：apple—/哀/；camel—/開/；Saturday —/塞/

原因辨析：

（1）口型未控制好，齒間間距過小。

（2）發音過程中口型有滑動；整個發音過程中，口型應保持在固定位置。

（3）發音時，舌尖未抵下齒、太靠后，齒間間距或過大，發音部位過於松弛。

（四）/æ/的發音練習

1. 單詞朗讀：

詞首	
an/æn，ən/一個	act/ækt/行為
apple/ˈæpl/蘋果	atom/ˈætəm/原子
absent/ˈæbsənt/缺席的	annual/ˈænjʊəl/每年的
anxious/ˈæŋkʃəs/焦慮的	avenue/ˈævɪnjuː/林蔭大道
actually/ˈæktʃʊəlɪ/事實上	atmosphere/ˈætməsfɪə/大氣
詞中	
bad/bæd/壞的	cap/kæp/帽子
fat/fæt/胖的	lack/læk/缺乏
matter/ˈmætə/事情	pattern/ˈpætən/樣式
national/ˈnæʃənəl/國家的	practical/ˈpræktɪkəl/實用的
romantic/rəˈmæntɪk/浪漫的	satisfactory/ˌsætɪsˈfæktərɪ/滿意的

2. 短語朗讀：

a bad habit 一個壞習慣	a happy family 一個幸福的家庭
as a matter of fact 事實上	carry a pan 攜帶一個平底鍋
stand back 往后站	hand in hand 手牽手
glad to be flattered 聽到別人的恭維很高興	
catch that mad black cat 抓住那只瘋狂的黑貓	
marry with the left hand 與門第比自己低的人結婚	
a traffic jam 交通堵塞	

3. 句子朗讀：

Fancy that!
真想不到！
A fact is a fact.
事實勝於雄辯。
Don't let the cat out of the bag.
不要洩露機密。
The man had a hammer in his hand.
那個男人手裡拿著錘子。
Alice and Agnes sat on the bank of a river.
艾麗斯和阿格尼絲坐在河岸上。

(五) 欣賞

1. 童謠：

I met a little boy Jack,
Who came from another land.
I couldn't speak his language,
But I took him by the hand.
To Acton and back,
On their narrow track.
The trains clang,
And rattle and bang,
And with angry crackles.
They sometimes scatter
Electric sparks
Above the clatter.

註：Acton：地名。clang：叮噹聲。rattle：（車輛）疾駛時發出的輪子的響聲。crackle：嚦啪聲。spark：火花。

2. 歌曲片段：

SAD SAD SAD

Fling you out into orbit
No one's going to hear you shout
And fools aren't going to follow
You don't need the sleaze about
Now you're sad sad sad
Sad sad sad
Sad sad sad

練習

1. 朗讀下列音素對比材料，注意對比音素的差異。

(1) /iː/ ↔ /ɪ/

bead	bid	meal	mill
bean	bin	meat	mitt
beat	bit	neat	knit
cheap	chip	peach	pitch
dean	din	peak	pick
deed	did	peel	pill
deep	dip	reach	rich
ease	is	reap	rip
feel	fill	seat	sit
field	filled	seek	sick
heal	hill	seen	sin
heat	hit	sleep	slip
jean	gin	sheep	ship
leap	lip	steal	still
least	list	teen	tin

(2) /ɪ/ ↔ /e/

bill	bell	pin	pen
chick	check	rid	red
him	hem	since	sense
knit	net	sinned	send
lid	led	sit	set
lint	lent	will	well
mint	meant	bin	Ben
pick	peck	wrist	rest

(3) /e/ ↔ /æ/

beck	back	fed	fad
bet	bat	guess	gas
end	and	led	lad

leg	lag	pen	pan
lend	land	said	sad
beg	bag	set	sat
merry	marry	then	than
mess	mass	step	stamp

(4) /iː/ ↔ /ɪ/ ↔ /e/ ↔ /æ/

bead	bid	bed	bad
bean	bin	Ben	ban
beat	bit	bet	bat
deed	did	dead	dad
dean	din	den	Dan
heed	hid	head	had
meat	mitt	met	mat
neat	knit	net	gnat
peak	pick	peck	pack
peter	pit	pet	pat
reek	Rick	wreck	rack
teen	tin	ten	tan

2. 辨認以下材料中的/iː/、/ɪ/和/i/，並正確朗讀。

(1) keep fit
(2) feel sick
(3) sweet lips
(4) a bit sweet
(5) a busy street
(6) keep to limits
(7) feed the baby
(8) greet the visitors
(9) leave the university
(10) fish in the sea
(11) deep in the river
(12) read it to me
(13) sit on the seat
(14) green with envy
(15) A pig is sleeping on a ship.
(16) Eat the fish, but don't eat the meat.
(17) A friend in need is a friend indeed.

第二節　單元音（2）：中元音

英語中元音的發音有如下共同特徵：①舌端離開下齒；②舌中部向上腭抬起，舌身平伸；③氣流未受到任何阻礙，沒有任何摩擦。

英語中元音的發音有如下漸變特徵：① /ɜː/、/ə/、/ʌ/的舌位由高到低，/ɜː/接近/e/，/ə/稍低，/ʌ/接近/æ/；② /ɜː/、/ə/、/ʌ/的開口程度由小到大。

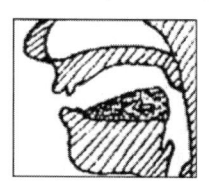

/ʌ/英式讀音符號

/ʌ/傳統的國際音標讀音符號

/ʌ/美式讀音符號

/ʌ/是字母 o，u 在單詞中的讀音。它是短元音。發音要領是舌尖和舌端兩側輕觸下齒，舌后部靠前部分稍抬起，唇形稍扁，開口度較大，與/æ/相似。

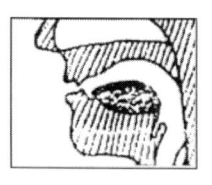

/ə/英式讀音符號

/ə/傳統的國際音標讀音符號

/ə/美式讀音符號

/ə/是字母 a，e，o，u，er，or，ur 在單詞中的讀音。它是短元音。發音要領是舌身平放，舌中部略隆起，雙唇扁平。

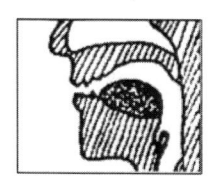

/ɜː/英式讀音符號

/əː/傳統的國際音標讀音符號

/əː/美式讀音符號

/ɜː/是字母組合 er，ir，or，ur 在單詞中的讀音。它是長元音。發音要領是舌中部比發/ə/音時略高，雙唇扁平。

一、/ʌ/

（一）/ʌ/的發音要領
/ʌ/的發音要領如圖 2-6 所示：

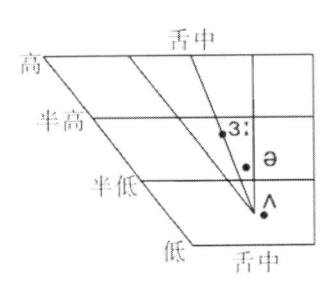

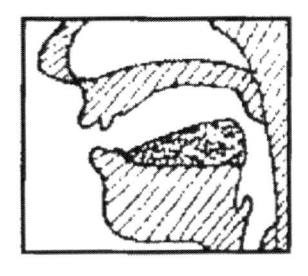

圖 2-6　中元音/ʌ/

發音部位：舌中部。
舌位：舌尖輕抵下齒，舌中部稍稍向上抬起。
口型：口要張大，和前元音/æ/的開口程度相似，雙唇向兩邊平伸成扁唇。
綜述：/ʌ/是短元音、中元音。發音時舌尖輕抵下齒，舌中部稍稍向上抬起；口要張大，和前元音/æ/的開口程度相似，雙唇向兩邊平伸成扁唇。

（二）/ʌ/的發音組合
1. 字母 u 在單詞中常常讀作/ʌ/。

| us | duck | ugly | must | under |
| up | drum | hurry | much | puddle |

2. 字母 o 在單詞中常常讀作/ʌ/。

| oven | love | other | lovely | welcome |
| come | onion | worry | colour | stomach |

3. 字母組合 ou 在單詞中常常讀作/ʌ/。

| tough | double | enough | couplet | flourish |
| touch | couple | country | doublet | courage |

4. 字母組合 oo 在單詞中偶爾讀作/ʌ/。

blood　　flood

（三）/ʌ/的常見發音錯誤辨析
常見錯誤：
（1）短元音長化：lovely—/ˈlaːvli/；us—/aːs/
（2）扁唇圓唇化：glove—/glaːv/
（3）母語化：讀成漢語的「啊」，如：summer 讀成/ˈsɑ mə/；love 讀成/辣 v/

原因辨析：

（1）唇型錯誤，嘴唇外延不夠。

（2）上下齒間間距過大。

（3）嘴角未繃緊。

（四）/ʌ/的發音練習

1. 單詞朗讀：

詞首	
up/ʌp/在……上面	until/ənˈtɪl, ʌnˈtɪl/直到……時
uncle/ˈʌŋkl/伯父；叔父	under/ˈʌndə/在……下面
unlock/ˈʌnˈlɒk/開啓	uncertain/ʌnˈsɜːtn/不（確）定的
uncover/ʌnˈkʌvə/揭開……的蓋子；揭露	undress/ˈʌnˈdres/使脫去衣服
umbrella/ʌmˈbrelə/傘	unusual/ʌnˈjuːʒʊəl/不常見的
詞中	
drug/drʌg/藥	truck/trʌk/卡車
jump/dʒʌmp/跳	number/ˈnʌmbə/數字
adjust/əˈdʒʌst/整理；調準	husband/ˈhʌzbənd/丈夫
hungry/ˈhʌŋgrɪ/饑餓的	lunch/lʌntʃ/午餐
summer/ˈsʌmə/夏季；壯年時期	front/frʌnt/前面
glove/glʌv/手套	monkey/ˈmʌŋkɪ/猴子；猿

2. 短語朗讀：

love each other 相愛	much money 很多錢
a very hard nut 一個難對付的人	enough bucks 有足夠的鈔票
hurry to make bucks 急趕著去掙錢	nothing so great 沒什麼了不起
tough enough 很難對付	no lust 沒有慾望
coming and going 來來往往	from cover to cover 從頭至尾

3. 句子朗讀：

Come to the front at the double.
快速到前面來。
The monkeys are funny.
這些猴子真有趣。
He hurried to the truck.
他趕緊跑到卡車那兒。
He loves nothing but money.
他只是愛錢。
She has enough money to repair the truck.
她有足夠的錢去修理那輛卡車。

(五) 欣賞

1. 繞口令：

Black bugs' blood.
Betty better butter Brad's bread.
Double bubble gum bubbles double.

2. 諺語：

The more noble, the more humble. 人越高尚，越謙虛。
The more wit, the less courage. 初生牛犢不怕虎。
It is not enough to do good; one must do it the right way. 人不僅要做好事，更要以正確的方式做好事。

3. 歌曲：

YOU WILL BE MY TRUE LOVE

You'll walk unscathed through musket fire,
No ploughman's blade will cut thee down,
No cutler's horn will mark thy face,
And you will be my true love,
And you will be my true love.
And as you walk through death's dark veil,
The cannon's thunder can't prevail,
And those who hunt thee down will fail,
And you will be my true love,
And you will be my true love.
Asleep inside the cannon's mouth,
The captain cries,「Here comes the rout,」
They'll seek to find me north and south,
I've gone to find my true love.
The field is cut and bleeds to red.
The cannon balls fly round my head,
The infirmary man may count me dead,
When I've gone to find my true love,
I've gone to find my true love.

二、/ə/

（一）/ə/的發音要領

/ə/的發音要領如圖 2-7 所示：

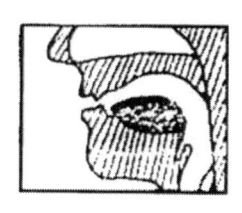

圖 2-7　中元音/ə/

發音部位：舌中部。
舌位：舌身放平，舌中部微微抬起。
口型：嘴唇微微張開，口腔自然放鬆發聲。
綜述：/ə/是短元音、中元音。發音時舌身放平，舌中部微微抬起；舌尖抵下齒；嘴唇微微張開，口腔自然放鬆發聲。

（二）/ə/的發音組合

1. 字母組合 er 在非重讀音節中常常讀作/ə/。

| tiger | sister | father | mother | brother |
| writer | lawyer | clever | manager | |

2. 字母組合 o(u)r 在非重讀音節中常常讀作/ə/。

| comfort | forget | forbid | horror | factor |
| favour | labour | humour | vapour | neighbour |

3. 字母 a 在非重讀音節中常常讀作/ə/。

| salad | formal | general | | |
| England | breakfast | formula | | |

4. 字母組合 ar 在非重讀音節中常常讀作/ə/。

| collar | scholar | regular | vinegar |
| similar | familiar | grammar | particular |

5. 字母 e 在非重讀音節中常常讀作/ə/。

| system | confidence | frequency | incident | accident |

6. 字母 o 在非重讀音節中常常讀作/ə/。

| confuse | police | polite |
| blossom | domestic | ceremony |

7. 字母 i 在非重讀音節中常常讀作/ə/。

| flexible | credible | visible |
| feasible | sensible | councilor |

8. 字母組合 ure 在非重讀音節中常常讀作 /ə/。

| future | picture | leisure | lecture | procedure |
| nature | injure | creature | gesture | adventure |

9. 字母組合 io 可讀作 /ə/，也可以不發音。

| nation | fashion | decision | question | information |
| ration | cushion | region | recession | registration |

10. 字母組合 ou 可讀作 /ə/。

| famous | curious | serious |
| courteous | courageous | harmonious |

11. 字母組合 ia 可讀作 /ə/，也可不發音。

| facial | partial | initial | essential | superficial |

(三) /ə/ 的常見發音錯誤辨析

常見錯誤：

（1）短元音長化：ruler—/ˈruːlɜ/；afternoon—/ˌʌftɜːˈnuːn/
（2）母語化：讀成漢語的「餓」；teacher—/ˈtiː 車餓/
（3）兒音化：讀成中文的「兒」或「而」，如：later—/ˈleɪt 兒/；arrive—/而 ˈraɪv/

原因辨析：

（1）唇型錯誤，嘴唇未外延或外延過度。
（2）發音部位錯誤地轉移到了齒齦，應為硬腭。
（3）舌位錯誤，把中元音變成了前元音。此外，不應該卷舌。

(四) /ə/ 的發音練習

1. 單詞朗讀：

詞首	
ago/əˈgəʊ/以前，已往	agree/əˈgriː/同意，贊成
ahead/əˈhed/早於	admit/ədˈmɪt/承認
about/əˈbaʊt/關於	afford/əˈfɔːd/擔負得起
abroad/əˈbrɔːd/在國外，到海外	advise/ədˈvaɪz/勸告
amaze/əˈmeɪz/使驚愕	afraid/əˈfreɪd/怕，害怕
詞中	
horizon/həˈraɪzn/平線；眼界	connect/kəˈnekt/連接
confuse/kənˈfjuːz/使混亂	economic/ˌiːkəˈnɒmɪk/經濟的
funeral/ˈfjuːnərəl/葬禮	machine/məˈʃiːn/機器；機械
company/ˈkʌmpənɪ/同伴；公司	elderly/ˈeldəlɪ/較老的
concert/ˈkɒnsət/音樂會	conference/ˈkɒnfərəns/協商

詞尾	
cinema/ˈsɪnɪmə/電影院	diploma/dɪˈpləʊmə/畢業文憑
pizza/ˈpiːtsə/比薩餅	camera/ˈkæmərə/攝影；照相機
colour/ˈkʌlə/顏色	honour/ˈɒnə/尊敬；敬重
daughter/ˈdɔːtə/女兒	farmer/ˈfɑːmə/農夫
carpenter/ˈkɑːpɪntə/木匠	fever/ˈfiːvə/發熱

2. 短語朗讀：

to suffer for one's wisdom 聰明反被聰明誤
gate-crasher 不速之客
around ten o'clock 大約在十點鐘
a Canadian businessman 一個加拿大商人
have a very formal talk 進行正式會談
forget to greet them 忘了和他們打招呼
a very bad car accident 一次惡性車禍
the federal government 聯邦政府
a committee member 委員會成員
the manager of the company 公司經理

3. 句子朗讀：

The farmer's sister is a doctor.
這個農民的姐姐是個醫生。
My brother's eating a hamburger merrily.
我弟弟正高興地吃著漢堡包呢。
It's a matter of time.
這只是一個時間的問題。
A good medicine tastes bitter.
良藥苦口。
A mother's love never changes.
母愛永恆。

(五) 欣賞

1. 繞口令：

A bitter biting bittern bit a better brother bittern, and the bitter better bittern bit the bitter biter back. And the bitter bittern, bitten, by the better bitten bittern, said,「I'm a bitter biter bit, alack！」

> Peter Piper picked a peck of pickled pepper prepared by his parents and put them in a big paper plate.
>
> A tutor who tooted a flue tried to tutor two tooters to toot. Said the two to their tutor, 「Is it harder to toot or to tutor two tooters to toot?」

2. 諺語：

> One never loses anything by politeness.
> 講禮貌不吃虧。
>
> Courage is the ladder on which all the other virtues mount.
> 勇氣是其他美德攀登的其他梯子。
>
> Wisdom in the mind is better than money in the hand.
> 腦中有知識，勝過手中有金錢。

3. 歌曲：

> **MOON RIVER**
> Moon river, wider than a mile,
> I'm crossing you in style some day.
> Oh, dream maker, you heart breaker,
> Wherever you're going, I'm going your way.
> Two drifters, off to see the world,
> There's such a lot of world to see.
> We're after the same rainbow's end,
> Waiting round the bend,
> My huckleberry friend, moon fiver, and me.

（六）語音小常識

1. 元音字母在非重讀音節中的讀音

字母	讀音	例詞	
a		go/gəʊ/以前	China/ˈtʃaɪnə/中國
o	/ə/	together/təˈgeðə/一起	second/ˈsekənd/第二
u		support/səˈpɔːt/支持	difficult/ˈdɪfɪkəlt/困難
e		before/bɪˈfɔː/以前	jacket/ˈdʒækɪt/上衣
i	/ɪ/	capital/ˈkæpɪtəl/首都	morning/ˈmɔːnɪŋ/早上
y		study/ˈstʌdɪ/學習	city/ˈsɪtɪ/城市

上表中提到的六個元音字母在非重讀音節中一般弱讀為/ə/或/ɪ/（見上表）。但在某些詞中也可以念作其他元音（見下表）。

字母	讀音	例詞
a	/ɪ/ /æ/ /eɪ/	comrade/ˈkɒmrɪd/同志 contrast/ˈkɒntræst/對比 celebrate/ˈselɪbreɪt/慶祝
e	/ə/ /e/	silent/ˈsaɪlənt/沉默 content/kənˈtent/內容
i（y）	/ə/ /aɪ/	holiday/ˈhɒlədɪ，ˈhɒlɪdeɪ/假日 organize/ˈɔːgənaɪz/組織 satisfy/ˈsætɪsfaɪ/滿足
o	/əʊ/	piano/pɪˈɑːnəʊ，ˈpjɑːnəʊ/鋼琴 potato/pəˈteɪtəʊ/白薯
u	/juː/ /u/	institute/ˈɪnstɪtjuːt/學院 instrument/ˈɪnstrʊmənt/儀器 conjugate/ˈkɒndʒʊgɪt/

2. 非重讀 r 音節的讀音規則

字母	讀音	例詞
ar er ir/yr or ur	/ə/	collar/ˈkɒlə/領子 grammar/ˈgræmə/語法 teacher/ˈtiːtʃə/教師 farmer/ˈfɑːmə/農民 tapir/ˈteɪpə/貘（動物） martyr/ˈmɑːtə/烈士 doctor/ˈdɒktə/醫生 forget/fəˈget/忘記 murmur/ˈmɜːmə/喃喃 Saturday/ˈsætədɪ/星期六

三、/ɜː/

（一）/ɜː/的發音要領

/ɜː/的發音要領如圖 2-8 所示：

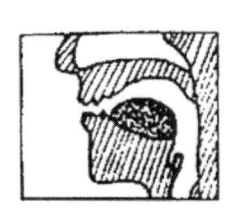

圖 2-8 中元音/ɜː/

發音部位：舌中部。
舌位：舌身平放，舌中部稍抬起。
口型：嘴型扁平，上下齒微開。
綜述：/ɜː/是長元音、中元音。發音時舌身平放，舌中部向上腭抬起，舌位接近/e/的高度；唇型扁平，向左右略微拉開；上下齒微開，比發/ə/音時略高。

(二) /ɜː/ 的發音組合

1. 字母組合 ur 在重讀音節中常常讀作 /ɜː/。

| hurt | turn | burn | curl | purse |
| curse | further | furnish | purple | purpose |

2. 字母組合 er 常常讀作 /ɜː/，尤其在重讀音節中。

| were | concern | deserve | expert | diverse |

3. 字母組合 ir 在重讀音節中常常讀作 /ɜː/。

| sir | bird | girl | skirt | circular |
| first | firm | circus | virtue | confirm |

4. 字母組合 or 在重讀音節中常常讀作 /ɜː/。

| work | word | world |
| worm | worse | worship |

5. 字母組合 ear 常常讀作 /ɜː/。

| yearn | earth | pearl |
| heard | learn | search |

(三) /ɜː/ 的常見發音錯誤辨析

常見錯誤：

(1) 長元音短化：birthday—/ˈbəθdei/
(2) 扁唇圓唇化或前趨化：bird—/bəd/；work—/wɔːk/
(3) 他音化：girl—/gʌl/
(4) 母語化：purple—/ˈ坡 pl/　hamburger—/ˈham 撥 gə/

原因分析：

(1) 發音長度不夠，舌身抬起偏低。
(2) 嘴唇外延不夠。
(3) 口型張開過大；嘴型扁平，上下齒微開即可。
(4) 發音時嘴部周圍肌肉過於鬆弛。

(四) /ɜː/ 的發音練習

1. 單詞朗讀：

詞首
urge /ɜːʤ/ 催促　　　　　　　　　urban /ˈɜːbən/ 城市的
urgent /ˈɜːʤənt/ 急迫的　　　　　Ursa /ˈɜːsə/【天】大熊座
earn /ɜːn/ 賺錢　　　　　　　　　early /ˈɜːlɪ/ 早期的
earl /ɜːl/ 伯爵　　　　　　　　　earnest /ˈɜːnɪst/ 認真的
Irwin /ˈɜːwɪn/ 歐文　　　　　　　erdin /ˈɜːdɪn/ 土曲霉素

詞中	
yearn/jɜːn/渴望，思念 nurse/nɜːs/保姆；護士 church/tʃɜːʃ/教堂 expert/ˈekspɜːt/專家，能手 dirty/ˈdɜːtɪ/髒的，不潔的 circuit/ˈsɜːkɪt/環行；電路 worst/wɜːst/最壞的，最惡劣的	burst/bɜːst/爆炸；突然發生 murder/ˈmɜːdə/凶殺，殺害 nervous/ˈnɜːvəs/不安的；膽怯的 concern/kənˈsɜːn/涉及，有關 shirt/ʃɜːt/襯衫；內衣 worship/ˈwɜːʃɪp/崇拜，禮拜 worth/wɜːθ/相當於……的價值
詞尾	
stir/stɜː/攪拌 defer/dɪˈfɜː/拖延 refer/rɪˈfɜː/委託；提到，指（的是） infer/ɪnˈfɜː/推測；猜想 fur/fɜː/軟毛；皮毛	confer/kənˈfɜː/商談，討論 her/hɜː, ˌhɜ, ə/她的 prefer/prɪˈfɜː/寧可，更喜歡 inter/ɪnˈtɜː/埋葬 blur/blɜː/模糊；斑點；不清晰

2. 短語朗讀：

work in a company 在一家公司工作 fell in love with a girl 愛上一個女孩兒 an American firm 一家美國公司 a bird in the hand 已經到手的東西 a long journey 一次長途旅行	serve in the army 當兵 work as a nurse 當護士 go to church 去教堂 a dirty shirt 一件髒裙子 show no mercy 毫無憐憫

3. 句子朗讀：

Thirty German girls were working in that firm for thirty years.
30個德國女子在那家公司工作了30年。
The early bird catches the worm (first).
早起的鳥兒有蟲吃。/笨鳥先飛。
He cursed the nurse for her bad service.
他咒罵了那個服務質量極差的護士。
Don't turn me down.
不要拒絕我。
The secret of success is constancy of purpose.
成功的秘訣在於目標堅定不移。

(五) 欣賞

1. 繞口令：

Urgent detergent!
Nine nice night nurses nursing nicely.
Dust is a disk's worst enemy.

2. 諺語：

Early to bed and early to rise makes a man healthy, wealthy and wise. 早睡早起使人健康、富有、明智。
Fire and water have no mercy. 水火無情。
Fools learn nothing from wise men, but wise men learn much from fools. 愚者不學無術，智者不恥下問。

3. 歌曲：

DREAM

I was a little girl alone in my little world,
who dreamed of a little home for me.
I played pretend between the trees,
and fed my houseguests bark and leaves,
and laughed in my pretty bed of green.
I had a dream
That I could fly from the highest swing.
I had a dream.
Long walks in the dark through woods grown behind the park,
I asked God who I'm supposed to be.
The stars smiled down on me,
God answered in silent reverie.
I said a prayer and fell asleep.

(六) 語音小常識：中元音小結

英語中有三個中元音，即/ʌ/、/ɜː/、/ə/。發中元音時舌位最高點在舌的中部，舌中部要稍稍抬起，例如/ɜː/，它的口形和前元音/e/相似，兩者的區別主要是舌位不同：/e/的發音在舌前部，/ɜː/的發音在舌中部。連續發/e/和/ɜː/這兩個元音就能感到發/e/時舌前部要使勁，發/ɜː/時則舌中部要使勁。/ə/的舌位和/ɜː/一樣，兩者在音質上無區別。但要注意兩點：① /ɜː/是長元音，/ə/是短元音；② /ɜː/在音節中一般都要重讀，發音十分清楚，/ə/在音節中永遠不重讀，

因而發音短促，較含糊，往往一帶而過。/ʌ/是中元音中的「后起之秀」，它在三個中元音中舌位最低，口形最大。

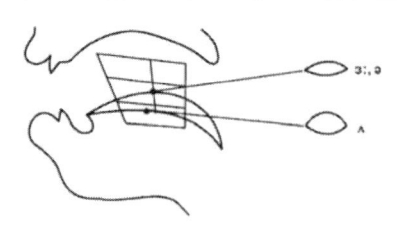

學習中元音時要注意/ʌ/的發音。/ɜː/和/ə/與漢語普通話中的 e（鵝）及輕聲的韻母 e 相似，不難學。中元音/ɜː/、/ə/、/ʌ/舌位區別如圖 2-9 所示：

圖 2-9　中元音/ɜː/、/ə/、/ʌ/舌位比較圖

（1）/ʌ/在過去的語音書中算作后元音，但根據 1972 年重版的 A. C. Gimson 的《英語發音辭典》中的單元音發音示意圖可以看到，/ʌ/的舌位已大大前移，由圖的中央線的右邊前移到中央線的左邊，/ʌ/的舌位甚至比中元音/ɜː/、/ə/還要靠前，因此只能允許/ʌ/在中元音裡安家落戶，稱其為「后起之秀」或「新秀」了。

（2）補充說明：最新版《英語發音辭典》（第 15 版）的單元音示意圖，/ʌ/又從上述位置倒退到和/ɜː/、/ə/的同一條垂直線上（見圖 2-10），英語元音的舌位變化真可謂「日新月異」！

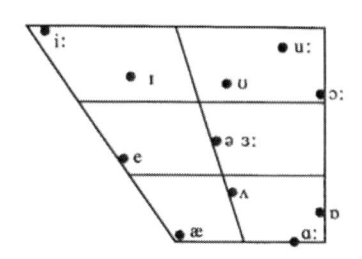

圖 2-10　第 15 版《英語發音辭典》上的 12 個單元音發音示意圖

練習

朗讀下列音素對比材料，注意對比音素的差異。

（1）/ɑː/↔/ʌ/

art	utter	lark	luck
fast	fuss	last	lust
mark	muck	smart	smut
harm	hum	staff	stuff

（2）/ɜː/ ↔ /ə/

inter	enter	worker	water
infer	offer	convert	cover
refer	referee	concern	concert
further	forbid	perfume	perform

第三節　單元音（3）：后元音

英語后元音的發音有如下共同特徵：①舌端離開下齒；②舌后部向上腭抬起，但不接觸；③氣流未受到任何阻礙，沒有任何摩擦。

英語后元音的發音有如下漸變特徵：① /uː/、/ʊ/、/ɔː/、/ɒ/、/ɑː/ 的舌位由高向低；② /uː/、/ʊ/、/ɔː/、/ɒ/、/ɑː/ 的開口程度由小到大。

一、/uː/

（一）/uː/的發音要領

/uː/的發音要領如圖 2-11 所示：

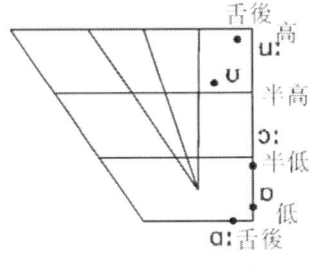

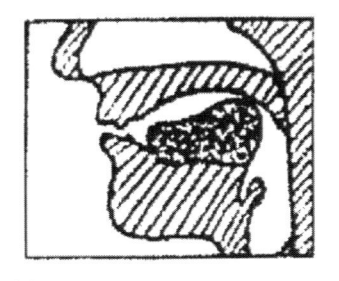

圖 2-11　后元音/uː/

發音部位：舌尖離開下齒。
舌位：舌身后縮，舌后部盡量向軟腭抬起。
口型：雙唇收圓並用力向前突出，口腔肌肉始終保持緊張，發長音。
綜述：/uː/是長元音、后元音。發音時舌尖離開下齒，舌身后縮，舌后部盡量向軟腭抬起；雙唇收圓並用力向前突出；長音。在5個后元音中，/uː/的舌位最高，口型最小。

（二）/uː/的發音組合

1. 字母 o 的讀音常常為/uː/，尤其在開音節中。

| whose | whom | who | move |
| tomb | movie | approve | lose |

2. 字母組合 oo 的讀音常常為/uː/。

| too | cool | school | bloom | room |

boot　　　　root　　　　noon　　　　spoon　　　　shoot

3. 字母 u 的讀音常常為/uː/。
rule　　　　June　　　　rumor　　　　crucial　　　　cruelty

4. 字母組合 ui 的讀音偶爾為/uː/。
juice　　　　fruit　　　　cruise　　　　recruit

5. 字母組合 ue 的讀音偶爾為/uː/。
blue　　　　true

6. 字母組合 ou 的讀音偶爾為/uː/。
wound

7. 字母組合 ough 的讀音偶爾為/uː/。
through

(三) /uː/的常見發音錯誤辨析

常見錯誤：

（1）長音短音化：root—/rʊt/；school—/skʊl/

（2）母語化：讀成中文的「烏」，如：too—/兔/；spoon—/s 不 n/

原因辨析：

（1）發音時間過短。

（2）發音時，舌身未后縮，舌后部未向軟腭抬起，發音部位過於松弛。雙唇阻礙氣流流出，加進一個輔音/w/，讀作/wu/。

(四) /uː/的發音練習

1. 單詞朗讀：

詞首	
ooze/uːz/滲出；慢慢流出 oozy/ˈuːzɪ/有淤泥的	oodles/ˈuːdlz/大量；巨額
詞中	
pool/puːl/水池 loose/luːs/松的；松散的 improve/ɪmˈpruːv/改善；改進 crucial/ˈkruːʃɪəl, ˈkruːʃəl/重要的 recruit/rɪˈkruːt/徵募新兵	mood/muːd/心情；情緒 prove/pruːv/證明；證實 rumor/ˈruːmə/謠言 cruise/kruːz/（軍艦等）巡邏；巡航 wound/wuːnd/傷口
詞尾	
do/duː/做 zoo/zuː/動物園 true/truː/真實的	who/huː/誰 blue/bluː/藍色的 through/θruː/通過；貫穿

2. 短語朗讀：

the full moon 滿月	fool-proof 萬無一失的，肯定成功的
pull out a tooth 拔牙	recruit new members 吸收新成員
in the moonlight 在月光下	a truly good book 一本很好的書
as soon as 立即，一……就	too good to be true 好得難以置信
move into the room 移進房間	look sb. through and through 仔細打量某人

3. 句子朗讀：

Soon learn, soon forgotten.
學得快，忘得快。
A fool's bolt is soon shot.
蠢人易於智窮。
The tooth became loose too soon.
牙齒很快變得鬆弛起來。

(五) 欣賞

1. 繞口令：

A tutor who tooted a flute tried to tutor two tooters to toot.
Said the two to their tutor,「Is it harder to toot or to tutor
two tooters to toot?」

2. 諺語：

A fool and his money are soon parted.
傻瓜存不住錢。

Sooner or later, the truth comes to light.
早晚真相會大白。

Losers are always in the wrong.
失敗者總是錯的。

What does the moon care if the dogs bark at her?
月亮豈怕狗來吠。

3. 童謠：

Hey, diddle, diddle, 嘿，快搖，快搖，
The cat and the fiddle, 貓咪和小提琴，
The cow jumped over the moon, 母牛跳過月亮，
The little dog laughed to see such sport, 看到此情景小狗哈哈笑，
And the dish ran away with the spoon. 碟子帶著湯匙不見了。

二、/ʊ/

(一) /ʊ/的發音要領

/ʊ/的發音要領如圖 2-12 所示：

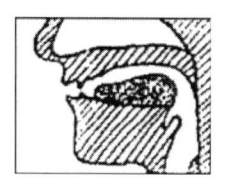

圖 2-12　后元音/ʊ/

發音部位：舌尖離開下齒。

舌位：舌身后縮，舌后部盡量向軟腭抬起；但舌位比/u:/稍低，是/u:/的對應短音。

口型：雙唇收圓並稍稍向前突出，開口程度比/u:/略大；發短音。

綜述：/ʊ/是短元音、后元音。發音時舌尖離開下齒，舌身后縮，舌后部盡量向軟腭抬起，但舌位比/u:/稍低；雙唇收圓並稍稍向前突出，開口程度比/u:/略大；短音。

(二) /ʊ/的發音組合

1. 字母組合 oo 的讀音常常為/ʊ/。

good　　　look　　　book　　　cook　　　hook
foot　　　wood　　　wool　　　took　　　hood

2. 字母 u 的讀音常常為/ʊ/。

put　　　bush　　　push　　　bull　　　full
pull　　　cruel　　　butcher　　sugar　　pudding

3. 字母組合 oul 的讀音常常為/ʊ/。

could　　　would　　　should

4. 字母 o 的讀音偶爾為/ʊ/。

wolf　　　woman

(三) /ʊ/的常見發音錯誤辨析

常見錯誤：

(1) 他音化：good—/gɜːd/；look—/lɜːk/。

(2) 短音長音化：should—/ʃuɜːd/。

(3) 母語化：讀成中文的「烏」，如：book—/不 k/；food—/負 d/。

原因辨析：

(1) 口型未控制好，齒間間距過小。

(2) 發音時間過長。

（3）發音時，舌身未后縮，舌后部未向軟腭抬起，發音部位過於松弛。雙唇阻礙氣流流出，加進一個輔音/w/，讀作/wu/。

（四）/ʊ/的發音練習

1. 單詞朗讀：

詞中	
hood/hʊd/頭巾；兜帽	hook/hʊk/鈎，釣鈎
crooked/ˈkrʊkɪd/彎曲的	cookie/ˈkʊkɪ/曲奇
bush/bʊʃ/灌木叢	bull/bʊl/公牛
butcher/ˈbʊtʃə/屠夫	wolf/wʊlf/狼
should/ʃʊd，ʃəd，ʃd/應該	

2. 短語朗讀：

a cook-book 一本烹調書	put to use 使用
a good loser 輸得起的人	go to school on foot 步行上學
put off 推遲；拖延	in the bushes 在灌木叢林中
the good wool 好的羊毛	no mood for reading the book 沒心情看書
put the wood on the table 把木頭放在桌子上	

3. 句子朗讀：

> You should make good use of that rare opportunity.
> 你應該好好利用這一次難得的機會。
> He polished his car till it looked like new.
> 他把他的車擦得跟新的一樣。
> I looked through the newspaper but I could not find any report on me accident.
> 我把報紙讀了個遍，也沒能找到任何關於那次車禍的報導。
> It would take a pretty clever person to pull the wool over his eyes.
> 要想蒙騙他，得找一個非常聰明的人才行。
> The cook took a spoon of sugar and put it in the food.
> 廚師取一小匙糖放進食物裡。

（五）欣賞

1. 繞口令：

> How many cookies could a good cook cook if a good cook could cook cookies? A good cook could cook as much cookies as a good cook who could cook cookies.

> I would if I could, and if I couldn't, how could I?
> You couldn't, unless you could, could you?

2. 諺語：

A good book is a good friend. 好書如摯友。
Look before you leap. 三思而行。
He that fears every bush must never go a-birding. 前怕狼后怕虎，當不了獵戶。
One beats the bush, and another catches the bird. 坐享別人的勞動成果。
He who keeps company with a wolf will learn to howl. 跟狼在一起，就會學狼叫。/近墨者黑。

三、/ɔː/

(一) /ɔː/的發音要領

/ɔː/的發音要領如圖 2-13 所示：

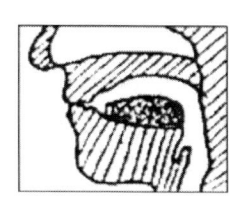

圖 2-13　后元音/ɔː/

發音部位：舌尖與下齒齊平。

舌位：舌身平放稍微后縮，舌尖稍稍用力，舌位比/ɑː/稍高。

口型：張開口，牙床開得較小，約為三分之二；雙唇稍稍收圓，並稍向前突出。

綜述：/ɔː/是后元音，長元音。在發音時張口要大，舌位比/ɑː/稍高，舌頭后縮，牙床半開，雙唇呈滾圓形，並稍向前突出。聲帶要振動，發長音。

(二) /ɔː/的發音組合

1. 字母組合 or 常常發后元音/ɔː/。

| oral | order | for | form | forty | lord |
| force | border | born | reform | report | |

2. 字母組合 al 常常發后元音/ɔː/。

| all | also | talk | walk | false |
| mall | hall | wall | small | salt |

3. 字母組合 aw 常常發后元音/ɔː/。
awful   awkward   crawl
draw   drawer   law

4. 字母組合 au 常常發后元音/ɔː/。
autumn   august   audience   cause
pause   cautious   assault   applaud

5. 字母 o 或字母組合 ore 在重讀音節中常常發后元音/ɔː/。
oral   story   storage   memorial   forecast
adore   bore   bored   more   before

6. 字母組合 our 和 oar 常常發后元音/ɔː/。
four   course   court
courtyard hoarse   hoard

7. 字母組合 ar 有時發后元音/ɔː/。
war   warn   warm
quarter   award   reward

8. 字母組合 oor 在詞尾偶爾發后元音/ɔː/。
door   floor

9. 字母 a 在 w 后面常常發后元音/ɔː/。
water   warn

10. 字母組合 au 有時發后元音/ɔː/。
author   laundry   launch

11. 字母組合 augh 有時發后元音/ɔː/。
taught   naught   naughty

(三)/ɔː/的常見發音錯誤辨析

常見錯誤：

(1) 長音短音化：story—/ˈstɒri/；four—/fɒ/

(2) 單元音雙元音化：如把 call 讀作/kaʊ/

(3) 母語化：讀成中文的「奧」或「襖」，如：law—/老/；more—/貓/

原因辨析：

(1) 發音時間過短。

(2) 發音過程中口型有滑動，實際上等於加進了一個/ʊ/或接近半元音/w/的音。

(3) 發音時，舌頭未后縮，雙唇未收圓，齒間間距或過大，發音部位過於松弛。

（四）/ɔː/ 的發音練習

1. 單詞朗讀：

詞首
oral /ˈɔːrə/ 口頭的；口述的　　orbit /ˈɔːbɪt/ 軌道 organ /ˈɔːgən/ 器官；元件　　ordinary /ˈɔːdɪnərɪ/ 普通的 already /ɔːlˈredɪ/ 已經，早已　　alternative /ɔːlˈtɜːnətɪv/ 兩者擇一的 authority /ɔːˈθɒrɪtɪ/ 權威；權勢　　automatic /ˌɔːtəˈmætɪk/ 自動的 awful /ˈɔːfʊl/ 可怕的　　awkward /ˈɔːkwəd/（手腳）不靈巧的
詞中
fortune /ˈfɔːtʃən/ 運氣；幸運　　resort /rɪˈzɔːt/ 求助；訴諸 coordinate /kəʊˈɔːdɪnɪt/ 協調　　chalk /tʃɔːk/ 粉筆；石灰石 halt /hɔːlt/ 停　　assault /əˈsɔːlt/ 攻擊 applaud /əˈplɔːd/ 鼓掌　　courtyard /ˈkɔːtjɑːd/ 庭院；院子 hoarse /hɔːs/ 刺耳的　　fault /fɔːlt/ 缺點；缺陷 crawl /krɔːl/ 向前慢慢爬　　warn /wɔːn/ 警告 water /ˈwɔːtə/
詞尾
for /fɔː, fə/ 為了　　war /wɔː/ 戰爭 shore /ʃɔː, ʃɒə/ 岸，濱　　score /skɔː, skɒə/ 記分 restore /rɪsˈtɔː/（使）恢復　　draw /drɔː/ 拉，拖 law /lɔː/ 法律　　door /dɔː, dɒə/ 門 floor /flɔː, flɒə/ 地面，地板　　adore /əˈdɔː/ 愛慕；敬重

2. 短語朗讀：

ought to 應該，必須　　law and order 法律和秩序 fill in a form 填寫表格　　father-in-law 岳父 what's more 而且　　more or less 或多或少 go forward 向前進　　the calm before the storm 暴風雨前的平靜

3. 句子朗讀：

Don't walk on the lawn. 不要在草坪上走。 Could you drop me off at the department store? 你能讓我在百貨公司下車嗎？ The army was called in to restore order. 部隊集合起來重整隊形。 I was bored to death by the boring job in the shop. 商店裡無聊的工作都快把我煩死了。 There are more and more social problems. 社會問題越來越多。

(五) 欣賞

1. 繞口令：

| She thought she ought to take a walk before four o'clock or draw balis and saws on the board. |
| Mr. See owned a saw and Mr. Soar owned a seesaw. Now, See's saw sawed Soar's seesaw before Soar saw See. |
| When a Walter doctors Water, does Walter doing the doctoring doctor as Water being doctored wants to be doctored or does Walter doing the doctoring doctor as he wants to doctor? |

2. 諺語：

| Losses make us more cautious. 損失使人更謹慎。 |
| Every man has his faults. 人非聖賢，孰能無過。 |
| A fault confessed is half redressed. 承認錯誤等於改正了一半。 |
| Faults are thick where love is thin. 一朝情義淡，樣樣不順眼。 |
| The drop hollows the stone, not by force but by the frequency of its fall. 滴水穿石不是由於使用強力所致，而是由於滴水頻繁所成。 |

四、/ɒ/

(一) /ɒ/的發音要領

/ɒ/的發音要領如圖 2-14 所示：

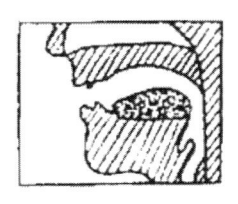

圖 2-14　后元音/ɒ/

發音部位：舌尖與下齒齊平。
舌位：舌身平放稍微后縮，舌后部抬起。
口型：/ɒ/在發音時口的開張度大於/ɔː/，牙床近乎全開，雙唇呈微圓形。

綜述：/ɒ/是后元音，短元音。在發音時口要張大，開張度大於/ɔː/，牙床近乎全開，雙唇稍稍收圓，聲帶要振動，發長音。

（二）/ɒ/的發音組合

1. 字母 o 常常發后元音/ɒ/。

office　　　　orange　　　　cock　　　　hot　　　　top
common　　　complex　　　forest　　　frog　　　royal

2. 字母 a 在字母 w 或字母組合 wh 后常常發后元音/ɒ/。

what　　　　wash　　　　watch　　　　want　　　　wander

3. 字母組合 ou 偶爾發后元音/ɒ/。

cough

（三）/ɒ/的常見發音錯誤辨析

常見錯誤：

（1）單元音雙元音化：operate—/'əʊpəreɪt/；modest—/'məʊdɪst/
（2）他音化：dog—/dʌg/；lust—/lʌst/
（3）母語化：讀成中文的「奧」如：top—/套 p/；job—/照 b/

原因辨析：

（1）發音過程中口型有滑動，舌頭未放平，並加進了一個/ʊ/。
（2）發音時，雙唇未收縮，口未張大。
（3）發音時，舌頭未后縮，雙唇未收圓，齒間間距或過大，發音部位過於松弛。

（四）/ɒ/的發音練習

1. 單詞朗讀：

詞首	
object/'ɒbdʒɪkt/物；物體	odd/ɒd/奇；單數的
operate/'ɒpəreɪt/操作；運轉	option/'ɒpʃən/選擇
opposite/'ɒpəzɪt/對面的；相反的	obstacle/'ɒbstəkl/障礙物
occupy/'ɒkjʊpaɪ/填滿；占用	office/'ɒfɪs/辦公室
詞中	
want/wɒnt/想要	lot/lɒt/許多
adopt/ə'dɒpt/採用；採納	conquer/'kɒŋkə/徵服；攻克
correspond/kɒrɪs'pɒnd/通信	dominate/'dɒmɪneɪt/支配；統治
conscious/'kɒnʃəs/意識到的	modest/'mɒdɪst/謹慎的；謙虛的

2. 短語朗讀：

coffee shop 咖啡店	hot water 熱水
draw lots 抽籤	cotton socks 棉襪
belong to 屬於	in honor of 為了紀念
drop in 走訪	in common 共同的
on a holiday 度假	

3. 句子朗讀：

To top it all, I lost my job.
更糟的是，我丟了我的工作。
There are four options in our college.
我們大學裡有四門選修科。
Could you drop me off at the department store?
你能讓我在百貨公司下車嗎？
Her father's opposition remained their only obstacle.
她父親的反對是他們唯一的障礙。
The blue sky belongs equally to us all.
藍天為人所共有。

(五) 欣賞

1. 繞口令：

The boss is putting the little fox in a big box.

All I want is a proper cup of coffee made in a proper copper coffee pot, you can believe it or not, but I just want a cup of coffee in a proper coffee pot. Tin coffee pots or iron coffee pots are of no use to me. If I can't have a proper cup of coffee in a proper copper coffee pot, I'll have a cup of tea!

Tie a knot, tie a knot, tie a tight knot, tie a knot in the shape of a naught.

2. 諺語：

Dog does not eat dog.
物不傷其類。

Barking dogs don't bite.
吠狗不咬人。

Love me, love my dog.
愛屋及烏。

Birds of a feather flock together. 物以類聚，人以群分。
To conquer or to die. 非勝即死。／不成功，便成仁。

五、/ɑː/

（一）/ɑː/的發音要領

/ɑː/的發音要領如圖 2-15 所示：

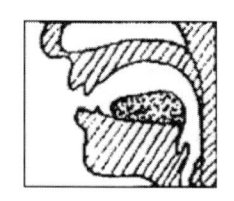

圖 2-15　后元音/ɑː/

發音部位：舌尖與下齒齊平。
舌位：舌位很低，舌身盡量低平，舌根部后縮。
口型：口要張大，雙唇稍微收縮。
綜述：/ɑː/是長元音、后元音。發音時把嘴張大，舌尖離開下齒，舌身平放並后縮，不要帶圓。聲帶振動，長度要發夠。

（二）/ɑː/的發音組合

1. 字母 a 常常發/ɑː/的音。

ask   task   pass   fast   staff
glass   class   aircraft   answer   commander

2. 字母組合 ar 在重讀音節中常常發/ɑː/的音。

art   arm   car   bar   farm
hard   card   star   smart   discard

3. 字母組合 al 常常發/ɑː/的音。

calm   palm

4. 字母組合 au 常常發/ɑː/的音。

laugh   laughter   aunt

5. 字母組合 ear 常常發/ɑː/的音。

heart   hearth   hearten

（三）/ɑː/的常見發音錯誤辨析

常見錯誤：

（1）圓唇扁唇化：answer—/ˈʌnsɜː/；laugh—/lʌf/
（2）他音化：calm—/kɔːm/；bar—/bɔː/；heart—/hɔːt/
（3）母語化：讀成中文的「啊」，如：car—/卡/；class—/k 拉 s/

原因辨析：

（1）發音時，口型未控制好，齒間間距過小。
（2）發音時，舌位靠前，雙唇收縮變圓。
（3）發音時，舌身靠前，未后縮，齒間間距或過大，發音部位過於松弛。

（四）/aː/的發音練習

1. 單詞朗讀：

詞首	
ask/ɑːsk/詢問；請求	answer/ˈɑːnsə/回答；答應
art/ɑːt/藝術；美術	arbitration/ˌɑːbɪˈtreɪʃən/仲裁；公斷
arm/ɑːm/胳膊	artist/ˈɑːtɪst/美術家；藝術家
argil/ˈɑːdʒɪl/陶土；礬土	argument/ˈɑːgjʊmənt/爭論；辯論
article/ˈɑːtɪkl/文章；論文	arctic/ˈɑːktɪk/北極的；寒帶的
詞中	
branch/brɑːntʃ/樹枝；分支	enhance/ɪnˈhɑːns/增強；增進
vast/vɑːst/巨大的；廣闊的	disaster/dɪˈzɑːstə/天災；災難
charge/tʃɑːdʒ/裝（滿）；充電	bark/bɑːk/犬吠
barber/ˈbɑːbə/（男）理髮師	margin/ˈmɑːdʒɪn/邊緣部分
marvelous/ˈmɑːvələs/不凡的	palm/pɑːm/手掌；掌心
詞尾	
bar/bɑː(r)/棒；條	car/kɑː/小汽車
mar/mɑː/毀損	far/fɑː/（空間，時間上）遠的
tar/tɑː/柏油；瀝青	star/stɑː/星星
scar/skɑː/傷疤；傷痕	cigar/sɪˈgɑː/雪茄菸

2. 短語朗讀：

pass the buck 推卸責任	come into the market 上市
make the mark 出人頭地	still in the dark 蒙在鼓裡
at the car park 在停車場	first-class management 一流的管理
pass the exam 通過考試	charge sb. with murder 指控某人謀殺
argue for/against 贊成/反對	a very smart fellow 一個很聰明的家伙

3. 句子朗讀：

> I'm waiting for you at the car park.
> 我在停車場等你。
> You have passed the exam; I am still in the dark.
> 你通過了考試，我還蒙在鼓裡呢。
> There is a vast grassland over there.
> 那邊有一個很大的草原。
> It will do a lot of harm to the heart.
> 這樣做對心臟的害處很大。
> What she has done is far from the mark.
> 她所做的一切離要求差得還很遠。

（五）欣賞

1. 繞口令：

> All artists are not artful.
> Oh, he passed a basket of grasses to the farms at half past nine last night.
> Master Carl asks his class not to go to the parks to play cards.

2. 童謠：

> Star light, star bright,
> First star I've seen tonight,
> I wish I may, I wish I might,
> Have the wish I wish tonight.

練習

1. 朗讀下列音素對比材料，注意對比音素的差異。
/ʌ/ ↔ /ɒ/ ↔ /ɜ/

son	song	society	other	occupy	occur
hut	hot	horizon	onion	obvious	obey
some	sorry	solution	comfort	comment	commit
oven	often	offend	company	competent	compare
fund	fond	forbid			

2. 朗讀以下音素 /ɑː/ 和 /ʌ/ 的對比材料，注意對比音素的差異。
發 /ɑː/ 音時，口要盡量張大，牙床全開，舌尖離開下齒，舌位放到最低點，

同時向后縮。發/ʌ/音時，舌頭在口腔裡平放著，舌面中部略抬起，牙床半開，舌位比中元音/aː/要低，肌肉松弛。練習這兩個音的時候，要特別注意它們之間的不同：① /aː/的舌位比/ʌ/后；② /aː/音口的開張度比/ʌ/大。

/ʌ/↔/aː/

tough	laugh	luggage	last
but	bark	glove	glass
touch	dark	love	laugh

3. 朗讀以下音素/ɔː/和/ɒ/的對比材料，注意對比音素的差異。

/ɔː/在發音時，舌頭后縮，牙床半開，雙唇呈滾圓形。/ɒ/在發音時舌面盡量壓低和往后靠，牙床近乎全開，呈微圓形。/ɒ/對中國學生來說是一個較難發好的音，許多人就用/ɔː/的短音來代替。為確保發音準確，請掌握這兩個元音的區別：① /ɒ/在發音時口的開張度大於/ɔː/，牙床近乎全開；② 發/ɔː/音時，雙唇呈滾圓形；發/ɒ/音時，雙唇呈微圓形。

/ɒ/↔/ɔː/

boss	ball	cop	cause
lock	lawn	fox	fall
not	naught	hot	halt
pot	pause	socks	saw
top	talk	watch	walk

4. 朗讀以下音素/uː/和/ʊ/的對比材料，注意對比音素的差異。

/uː/和/ʊ/都是高元音、后元音、圓唇元音。/uː/在英語后元音中，舌位是最高的。就如/iː/在前元音中舌位最高一樣。發此音時，舌頭后縮，並向軟腭隆起。這個音在當今世界的許多語言中都很常見，對大多數中國學習者來說，發此音並沒有多大問題。/ʊ/在發音時與/uː/一樣，舌頭后縮，但后縮程度不及/uː/，舌面隆起但程度不及/uː/。另外，發/ʊ/音時，肌肉的緊張程度不及/uː/。練習/uː/和/ʊ/的發音時，要特別注意以下幾點：① /uː/是舌位最高的后元音，因此舌頭隆得比/ʊ/音高；② 發/uː/音時，舌頭隆起部位比/ʊ/更接近舌根；③ 發/uː/音時，雙唇呈滾圓形；發/ʊ/音時，雙唇呈微圓形；④ 發/uː/音時，肌肉緊張度高，而發/ʊ/時，肌肉較為松弛。

/uː/↔/ʊ/

cool	cook	root	rook
goose	good	too	to
loose	look	soup	soot
noon	nook	woo	wood

第四節 雙元音（1）：合口雙元音

一、/eɪ/

/eɪ/的發音要領如圖 2-16 所示：

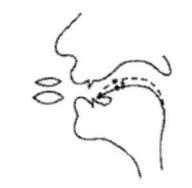

圖 2-16 雙元音/eɪ/

發雙元音/eɪ/時口形由/e/向/ɪ/滑動，發音過程中下巴稍向上合攏，舌位也隨之稍稍抬高。

發雙元音時尚須注意前重后輕、前長后短等特點（詳見本課語音小常識）。這些特點在學習八個雙元音時均須注意。

（一）Words 單詞

a plate   a radio
a table   a cake
a spade   a basin
an ashtray   a beefsteak

（二）Questions and Answers 問答

(1) Whose ashtray is this?
這是誰的菸灰缸？
It's mine. It's my ashtray.
是我的。這是我的菸灰缸。
(2) Whose beefsteak is this?
這是誰的牛排？
It's yours. It's your beefsteak. Eat it while it's still hot.
你的，是你的牛排。快趁熱吃。
(3) Whose transistor radio is this?
這是誰的半導體收音機？
It's hers. It's Jane's transistor radio. She likes to listen to the English radio programs.
她的。是簡的半導體收音機。她喜歡收聽英語廣播節目。
(4) Whose dinner table is that?
那是誰的飯桌？

It's ours. It's our dinner table.

我們的，是我們的飯桌。

（5）Whose birthday cake is this?

這是誰的生日蛋糕？

It's John's. It's his birthday cake. John is eighteen today. A happy birthday to John!

是約翰的生日蛋糕。今天是他18歲生日。祝約翰生日快樂！

（6）Whose washbasin is that?

那個洗臉盆是誰的？

It's ours. It's our new washbasin. Kate bought it for David's birthday.

是我們的。是我們的新洗臉盆。是凱特送給戴維的生日禮物。

（三）Dialogues 對話

（1）

A：We're going to see a Shakespeare's play today.

今天我們去看一場莎士比亞戲劇。

B：But what should I wear?

我穿什麼衣服？

A：Your pale grey dress, Amy. It's my favourite.

穿淡灰色的連衣裙，埃米。我最喜歡那件了。

B：But I can't wear the same dress day after day, Raymond. And anyway, the waist's too big.

但我不能天天穿同樣的裙子，雷蒙德。而且那件的腰太大了。

A：Mrs. Taylor is a good dressmaker. She can...

泰勒太太是個好裁縫，她能……

B：She can make me a new dress.

她能給我做件新衣服。

A：Wait a minute, Amy! I didn't say a new...

等等，埃米，我可沒說給你做新（衣服）……

（2）

A：Oh, may I stay, Mummy? Please say I can stay all day.

哦，媽，我能留下來嗎？告訴我我可以呆一整天。

B：Yes, if they say you may.

是的，如果他們同意的話。

A：They've got lots of places to play, and they've...

他們有好些地方可以去玩，而且他們……

B：Wait, Jane!

等等，簡！

A：I'll take my painting book, and some of my games.
我想帶著我的繪畫書和一些玩的東西。

B：Wait till they say you may.
你得等他們表示同意（讓你留下來）。

（四）New Words and Expressions 生詞和短語

1. 單詞朗讀：

plate/pleɪt/盤子	table/ˈteɪbl/桌子
spade/speɪd/鐵	ashtray/ˈæʃtreɪ/菸灰缸
radio/ˈreɪdɪəʊ/收音機	cake/keɪk/蛋糕
basin/ˈbeɪs(ə)n/臉盆	beefsteak/ˈbiːfsteɪk/牛排
whose/huːz/誰的	mine/maɪn/我的
yours/jɔːz, jʊəz/你（們）的	while/(h)waɪl/當……的時候
still/stɪl/還，仍	hot/hɒt/熱
transistor/trænˈzɪstə/半導體	listen/ˈlɪsn/秒. 聽

English/ˈɪŋglɪʃ/英語	dinner/ˈdɪnə/正餐
birthday/ˈbɜːθdeɪ/生日	eighteen/ˈeɪˈtiːn/十八
today/təˈdeɪ/今天	happy/ˈhæpɪ/快樂
ours/ˈaʊəz/我們的	buy/baɪ/買，購買
see/siː/看見	wear/weə/穿
pale/peɪl/淡的	grey/greɪ/灰色
favourite/ˈfeɪvərɪt/心愛之物	same/seɪm/同樣的
dress/dres/女服，連衣裙	anyway/ˈenɪweɪ/不管怎樣
waist/weɪst/腰	big/bɪg/大
Mrs. /ˈmɪsɪz/夫人	dressmaker/ˈdresmeɪkə(r)/（女裝）裁縫
play/pleɪ/話劇，戲劇	wait/weɪt/等候
minute/ˈmɪnɪt/分鐘	

2. 短語朗讀：

dinner table 餐桌	listen to... 聽……
wait a minute 等一下	day after day 天天，連著好幾天

（五）語音小常識：雙元音

英語裡共有八個雙元音，即/eɪ/、/əʊ/、/aɪ/、/aʊ/、/ɔɪ/、/ɪə/、/eə/、/ʊə/。前面五個叫做合口雙元音，因為其中第二個元音是合口元音/ɪ/或/ʊ/（見圖2-17）；后面三個叫集中雙元音，因為其中第二個元音都是中元音/ə/（見圖2-18）。

英語雙元音具有五個共同的特點：

（1）口形舌位有變化。發單元音時口形舌位自始至終保持不變。雙元音是

由兩個不同的元音組成的，例如/aɪ/，從第一個元音/a/過渡到/ɪ/，口形和舌位都有變化：由口形較大、舌位較低的/a/音過渡到口形較小、舌位較高的/ɪ/音。其他七個雙元音也一樣，發音時口形舌位都有不同程度的明顯變化。

（2）前長後短。雙元音中兩個元音的長度（音長）也不相等。第一個比第二個長些，約為三比一。

（3）前重後輕。發第一個元音時要多使點勁兒，發第二個元音則可以少使點勁兒，但必須注意不要把兩個元音分裂成一個強音、一個弱音來念，而是由強而漸弱。

（4）兩音密合，一氣呵成。由第一個元音到第二個元音是一個滑動的過程，中間不容停頓，不可把兩個音分開來念。

（5）前音清楚，後音模糊。雙元音中的第一個元音發音清楚響亮，向第二個音滑動時，在尚未到達第二個元音的發音部位時滑動即可停止，不必把第二個音念得像單獨發音時那麼清楚。這一點非常重要。常聽到一些同學把/aɪ/念成「阿姨」，就是因為把/ɪ/念得太清楚了，甚至跑過了頭，越境而入/iː/的領域了。

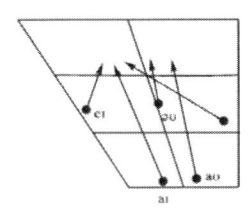

圖 2-17 英語合口雙元音示意圖
第 15 版《英語發音辭典》

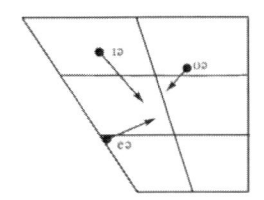

圖 2-18 英語集中雙元音示意圖
第 15 版《英語發音辭典》

練習

1. 朗讀下列單詞，注意/eɪ/和/e/的區別。

/eɪ/	/e/	/eɪ/	/e/
age 年齡	edge 邊緣	pain 疼痛	pen 鋼筆
mate 夥伴	met 預見	wait 等待	wet 濕
late 遲（到）	let 讓	waste 浪費	west 西
main 主要的	men 男人	gate 大門	get 拿，取

2. 朗讀下列短語和句子，注意雙元音/eɪ/的發音。

a radio on the table 桌上的一只收音機	a cake on the plate 盤中的一個蛋糕
the same day 同一天	Raymond's favourite 雷蒙德最喜愛的束西
Amy's great day 埃米重要的一天	Kate's grey bracelet 凱特的灰色手鐲
Taylor's late. 泰勒遲到了。	wait for May 等梅（小姐）

3. 朗讀下列小詩，注意/eɪ/的正確發音。

(1)

> In merry month of May,
> All the little birds are gay.
> They hop and sing and say.
> Winter days are far away,
> Welcome, welcome, merry May.

(2)

> Evening red and morning grey,
> Send the traveller on his way;
> Evening grey and morning red,
> Bringing the rain upon his head.

二、/əʊ/

/əʊ/的發音要領如圖 2-19 所示：

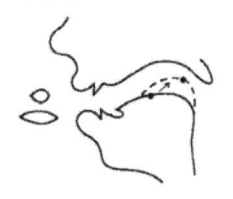

圖 2-19　雙元音/əʊ/

發雙元音/əʊ/時口形由中元音/ə/向后元音/ʊ/滑動，開始時的口形是扁平唇，結束時的口形是合圓唇。

注意防止把第二個元音念成/uː/或漢語普通話「烏」。

(一) Words 單詞

a boat　　　a sparrow
a goat　　　a potato
a bowl　　　a tomato

(二) Questions and Answers 問答

(1) Where's the boat?
小船在哪兒？
The boat? It's on the river.
小船？在河上。
The boat is on the river.

小船在河上。

（2）Where's the goat?

山羊在哪兒？

The goat? It's in the boat.

山羊？在船上。

The goat is in the boat.

山羊在船上。

（3）Where's the bowl?

碗在哪兒？

The bowl? It's on the radio.

碗？在收音機上。

The bowl is on the radio.

碗在收音機上。

（4）Where's the sparrow?

麻雀在哪兒？

The sparrow? It's up in the tree.

麻雀？在樹上。

The sparrow is up in the tree.

麻雀在樹上。

（5）Where are the potatoes and tomatoes?

土豆、西紅柿在哪兒？

The potatoes and tomatoes? They are in the big bowl.

土豆和西紅柿？在大碗裡。

The potatoes and tomatoes are in the big bowl over there.

土豆和西紅柿在那邊的大碗裡。

（三）Dialogues 對話

（1）

A：Now my dear Rose, tonight I'll make you a dinner. You'll have a rest. Close your eyes and listen to the radio. And tomorrow, we'll go to the Summer Palace to row a boat.

親愛的羅斯，今晚我來做飯，你休息一下。閉上眼睛聽聽廣播。明天我們去頤和園划船。

……

A：Rose, where are the potatoes?

羅斯，土豆在哪裡？

B：Yes, Joe? What do you want?

喬，你想要什麼？

A：Potatoes. Where are the potatoes?

要土豆。土豆在哪裡？

B：They are in the bag under the table.

在桌子下邊的包裡。

A：Oh, the bag under the table.

哦，在桌子下邊的包裡。

Rose, where are the tomatoes?

羅斯，西紅柿在哪裡？

B：The tomatoes? They are in the bowl in the cupboard.

西紅柿？在碗櫃的碗裡。

A：Rose, where's...

羅斯，哪裡有……

B：The meat?

肉？

A：Yes.

對。

B：I told you to buy it on your way home.

我不是告訴你在回家的路上要買肉嗎？

A：I forgot it.

我忘了。

B：Well, then, it's at the grocer's.

那就去食品店買肉吧！

A：OK. I'll go and get it.

好吧，我去買。

B：No, you won't. It's closed. The grocer's closed. It won't open until tomorrow morning.

不行，你買不到肉了。已經關門了。食品店已經關門了。要到明天上午才開門。

(2)

Listen to the two small children while they are playing.

下面是兩個小孩在做遊戲時的對話。

A：That's my comb.

這是我的梳子。

B：No, that's my comb.

不，這是我的梳子。

A：Where did you find the comb.

你在哪兒找到這把梳子的？

B：I found it in your coat.
在你上衣裡。

A：That's my boat.
這是我的小船（玩具）。

B：No, that's my boat.
不，這是我的小船。

A：Where did you find the boat?
你在哪兒找到這小船的?

B：I found it on the road.
在馬路上。

A：That's my notebook.
這是我的筆記本。

B：No, that's my notebook.
不，這是我的筆記本。

A：Where did you find it?
你在哪兒找到筆記本的?

B：I found it in mother's coat.
在媽媽的上衣裡。

A：That's my postcard.
這是我的明信片。

B：No, that's my postcard.
不，這是我的。

A：Where did you find it?
你在哪兒找到的?

B：I found it in father's coat.
在爸爸的上衣裡。

（四）New Words and Expressions 生詞和短語

1. 單詞朗讀:

boat/bəʊt/小船	goat/gəʊt/山羊
bowl/bəʊl/碗	sparrow/ˈspærəʊ/麻雀
potato/pəˈteɪəʊ/土豆	tomato/təˈmɑːtəʊ/西紅柿
on/ɒn/在……上	river/ˈrɪvə/河
radio/ˈreɪdɪəʊ/收音機	up/ʌp/在上面
tree/triː/樹	over/ˈəʊvə/在……上方
now/naʊ/現在	dear/dɪə/親愛的
my/maɪ/我的	tonight/təˈnaɪt/今晚
rest/rest/休息	close/kləʊz/閉合

eye/aɪ/眼睛	tomorrow/təˈmɒrəʊ, tʊˈmɒrəʊ/明天
row/raʊ/划（船）	under/ˈʌndə/在……下面
cupboard/ˈkʌbəd/碗櫃（櫥）	tell/tel/告訴，講
way/weɪ/道路	home/həʊm/家
forget/fəˈget/忘記	grocer/ˈgrəʊsə/食品雜貨店
open/ˈəʊpən/開（門）	till/tɪl/直到
small/smɔːl/小	children/ˈtʃɪldrən/小孩
comb/kəʊm/梳子	find/faɪnd/找到
coat/kəʊt/上衣	road/rəʊd/路
notebook/ˈnəʊtbʊk/筆記本	postcard/ˈpəʊstkɑːd/明信片

2. 短語朗讀：

up in the tree 在樹上	over there 在那邊
the Summer Palace 頤和園	on your way home 在你回家的路上

（五）語音小常識：元音的發音長度

英語裡的五個單元音/iː/、/ɑː/、/ɔː/、/uː/、/ɜː/和八個雙元音/eɪ/、/aɪ/、/ɔɪ/、/aʊ/、/əʊ/、/ɪə/、/eə/、/ʊə/都是長元音。這些元音都比短元音念得長，但在下面幾種情況下其發音長度略有不同：

（1）同一個重讀的長元音在詞末時比在以輔音結尾的詞末前念得長些。例如：

在詞末時元音長	在以輔音結尾的詞末前的元音短
go/gəʊ/去	goat/gəʊt/山羊
car/kɑː/小汽車	cart/kɑːt/大車
see/siː/看見	seat/siːt/座位

（2）同一個重讀長元音在濁輔音前比在清輔音前念得長一些。例如：

濁輔音前的元音長	清輔音前的元音短
leave/liːv/離開	leaf/liːf/葉子
male/meɪl/男性	make/meɪk/做
feed/fiːd/喂	feet/fiːt/腳

（3）同一個重讀長元音在單音節詞中比在兩個音節（或多音節）詞中念得長些。例如：

單音節中的元音長	雙（多）音節中的元音短
ask/ɑːsk/問	asking/ˈɑːskɪŋ/問
see/siː/看	seeing/ˈsiːɪŋ/看
lose/luːz/丟失	loser/ˈluːzə/失主

（4）同一個長元音在重讀音節中比在非重讀音節中念得長些。例如：

元音長（在重讀音節中）　　　元音短（在非重讀音節中）
verb/vɜːb/動詞　　　　　　　　adverb/ˈædvɜːb/副詞
record/ˈrekɔːd/錄音　　　　　　record/ˈrekɔːd/記錄

上面選擇了一些較為基本的有關元音長度的規則供讀者參考。限於篇幅，有關元音的發音長度在句中的情況就不一一列舉了。

練習

1. 朗讀下列單詞，注意單元音/ɔː/和雙元音/əʊ/之間的區別。

/əʊ/	/ɔː/	/əʊ/	/ɔː/
no 不	nor 也不	low 低	law 法律
bowl 碗	ball 球	coal 煤	call 打電話
coat 上衣	caught 捕捉	boat 小船	bought 買

2. 朗讀下列短語及句子，注意/əʊ/的讀音。

```
go home 回家              so lonely 這樣孤獨
hope so 希望如此          so cold 這麼冷
don't know 不知道         go to the grocery 去食品雜貨店
Oh, don't go home alone, Joan. 瓊，別獨自回家。
Little strokes fell great oaks. 滴水穿石（英諺）。
As you sow, you shall mow. 種瓜得瓜，種豆得豆（英諺）。
A straw will show which way the wind blows. 草動知方向（英諺）。
```

3. 朗讀下列對話，注意包含雙元音/əʊ/的單詞的發音：

A：I'm going to the post-office. Anything I can do for you, Rose?
　　我要去郵局，有什麼事要我做嗎，羅斯？

B：To the post-office? Can you get me some post-cards?
　　去郵局？能幫我買些明信片嗎？

A：OK. How many post-cards do you want?
　　可以。你想買多少？

B：Ten, please. By the way, I'm going to the grocery. Can I get you something?
　　要十個。順便告訴你，我要去雜貨店。你想買什麼東西嗎？

A：Yes. Could you get me some potatoes and tomatoes?
　　是的。能給我買些土豆和西紅柿嗎？

B：That's easy. OK. I'd better go now. The grocery closes at 5.
　　小事一件。我最好現在就去。食品店五點鐘關門。

A：The post-office also closes at 5. So why don't we go together?
　　郵局也是五點關門。咱們幹嗎不一起去？

三、/aɪ/

/aɪ/的發音要領如圖 2-20 所示：

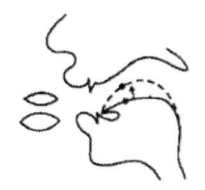

圖 2-20　雙元音/aɪ/

發英語雙元音/aɪ/時由舌位低、口形大的前元音/a/（此音只在雙元音/aɪ/、/aʊ/中使用）向舌位高、口形小的/ɪ/滑動。發音時舌尖要抵住下齒。

（一）Words 單詞

a kite　　　　　a meat pie
s knife　　　　a bike
an icecream　　a typewriter
a pipe　　　　 a lighter

（二）Questions and Answers 問答

A：How many kites are there in the sky?
　　天空中有幾只風箏？
B：Two. There're two kites in the sky.
　　兩只。天空中有兩只風箏。
A：How many knives are there on the table?
　　桌子上有幾把刀？
B：Three. There're three knives on the table.
　　三把。桌上有三把刀。
A：How many icecreams are there in the fridge?
　　冰箱裡有多少冰淇淋？
B：Nine. There're nine icecreams in the fridge.
　　九個。冰箱裡有九個冰淇淋。
A：How many meat pies are there on the plate?
　　盤子裡有幾個肉餡餅？
B：Six. There are six meat pies on the plate.
　　六個。盤子裡有六個肉餡餅。
A：How many pipes are there on the table?
　　桌子上有幾個菸鬥？
B：Five. There're five pipes on the table.

五個。桌上有五個菸鬥。

A：How many typewriters are there on the desk?
　　書桌上有幾個打字機？

B：Two. There're two typewriters on the desk.
　　兩個。書桌上有兩個打字機。

A：How many lighters are there in the box?
　　盒子裡有幾個打火機？

B：Three. There're three lighters in the box.
　　三個。盒子裡有三個打火機。

(三) Dialogue 對話

A：Are you seeing Mike tonight?
　　你今晚去見邁克嗎？

B：Yes. He has a new motorcycle.
　　是的，他買了一輛新摩托車。

A：Did Mike let you ride it?
　　邁克讓你騎他的車了嗎？

B：Yes. I tried it. And I liked it.
　　是啊，我試騎了一下，我喜歡他的車。

A：Were you frightened?
　　你騎車時害怕了嗎？

B：Sure. But I still liked it.
　　沒錯。但我還是喜歡他那輛摩托。

A．Would you like to buy a motorcycle?
　　你也想買輛摩托車嗎？

B：No, I don't think so. I think I'll buy a bike.
　　不，我不想買摩托車。我想買輛自行車。

A：A bike?
　　買自行車？

B：Yeah. Riding on Mike's motorcycle was nice, but I'd rattler have a bike.
　　是啊！騎邁克的摩托車的確不錯，不過我還是買自行車為好。

A：Why?
　　為什麼？

B：It's cheaper and safer. I don't want to die on a motorcycle.
　　自行車便宜多了，又安全。我不想騎摩托摔死。

（四）New Words and Expressions 生詞和短語

1. 單詞朗讀：

kite/kaɪt/風箏	knife/naɪf/刀子
pipe/paɪp/菸斗	pie/paɪ/帶餡的餅、派
bike/baɪk/自行車	typewriter/ˈtaɪpraɪtə/打字機
lighter/ˈlaɪtə/打火機	many/ˈmenɪ/多，許多
sky/skaɪ/天空	fridge/frɪdʒ/冰箱
motorcycle/ˈməʊtəsaɪkl/摩托車	ride/raɪd/騎
try/traɪ/試	frighten/ˈfraɪtn/害怕
sure/ʃʊə/肯定的，無疑的	so/səʊ/那樣，這樣
nice/naɪs/美好的	cheap/tʃiːp/便宜
safe/seɪf/安全的	die/daɪ/死

2. 短語朗讀：

meat pie 肉餡餅	how many...? 多少……？

（五）語音小常識：某些元音字母組合的讀音規則

元音字母（a, e, i, o, u, y）可以由兩個或三個元音字母一起構成一些字母組合。這些字母組合的讀音只能靠具體記憶來掌握。下面我們將提供一組比較常見的兩個字母組合在一起時的讀音規則（見表 2-1）。掌握並記住這些規則對學習英語語音及拼寫規律都會有很大幫助。

表 2-1　　　　　某些元音字母組合的讀音規則

字母組合	在重讀音節中的讀音		在非重讀音節中的讀音	
ai	/eɪ/ /e/	aid/eɪd/幫助 said/sed/說（過去式）	/ɪ/	portrait/ˈpɔːtrɪt/肖像
au	/ɔː/ /ɑː/	autumn/ˈɔːtəm/秋天 aunt/ɑːnt/姑母	/ə/	authority/ɔːˈθɒrɪtɪ/權力
ay	/eɪ/ /e/	day/deɪ/日子 says/sez/說（第三人稱）	/ɪ/	Sunday/ˈsʌndɪ/星期天
ea	/iː/ /eɪ/ /e/ /ɪə/	sea/siː/海 great/greɪt/偉大的 head/hed/頭 theatre/ˈθɪətə/戲院	/ɪ/	forehead/ˈfɒrɪd/前額
ee	/iː/	meet/miːt/遇見	/ɪ/	coffee/ˈkɒfɪ/咖啡
ei	/iː/ /aɪ/ /e/	ceiling/ˈsiːlɪŋ/天花板 either/ˈaɪðə(r)/也 leisure/ˈleʒə, ˈliːʒə/空閒	/ɪ/	foreign/ˈfɒrɪn/外國

表2-1(續)

字母組合	在重讀音節中的讀音		在非重讀音節中的讀音	
eo	/iː/ /e/	people/ˈpiːpl/人民 leopard/ˈlepəd/豹	/ə/	surgeon/ˈsɜːdʒən/ 外科醫生
eu	/juː/ /jʊə/	feudal/ˈfjuːdl/封建的 Europe/ˈjʊərəp/歐洲		
ey	/eɪ/ /iː/	they/ðeɪ, ðe/他們 key/kiː/鑰匙	/ɪ/	money/ˈmʌnɪ/錢
ia	/aɪə/	dialogue/ˈdaɪəlɒg/對話	/ə/	parliament/ˈpɑːləmənt/國會
ie	/iː/ /aɪ/ /e/	field/fiːld/田 die/daɪ/死 friend/frend/朋友	/ɪ/	auntie/ˈɑːntɪ/姑母
io	/aɪə/	pioneer/ˌpaɪəˈnɪə/少先隊員	/ɪə/	patriot/ˈpeɪtrɪət/愛國者
oa	/əʊ/ /ɔː/	coal/kəʊl/煤 broad/brɔːd/寬		
oe	/əʊ/ /uː/	hoe/həʊ/鋤 shoe/ʃuː/鞋子		
oi	/ɔɪ/	oil/ɔɪl/油	/ə/	tortoise/ˈtɔːtəs/烏龜
oo	/ʊ/ /uː/ /ʌ/	book/bʊk/書 too/tuː/也 blood/blʌd/血	/uː/	cuckoo/ˈkʊkuː/布穀鳥
ou	/uː/ /ʊ/ /ʌ/ /ɒ/	youth/juːθ/青年 could/kʊd/能 country/ˈkʌntrɪ/國家 cough/kɔːf/咳嗽	/ə/	courageous/kəˈreɪdʒəs/ 勇敢的
oy	/ɔɪ/	boy/bɔɪ/男孩		
ua	/jʊə/ /ʊə/	mutual/ˈmjuːtjʊəl, ˈmjuːtʃʊəl/互相 usual/ˈjuːʒʊəl/通常		
ue	/juː/ /uː/	due/djuː/由於 blue/bluː/藍色		
ui	/uː/ /juː/ /ɪ/	fruit/fruːt/水果 suit/sjuːt/合適 build/bɪld/建立		
uy ye	/aɪ/ /aɪ/	buy/baɪ/買 dye/daɪ/染		

第二章 元音

練習

1. 朗讀下列單詞，注意區別雙元音/aɪ/和單元音/æ/的不同發音。

/aɪ/	/æ/	/aɪ/	/æ/
right 右	rat 鼠	height 高度	hat 帽子
side 旁邊	sad 悲傷	fight 打架	fat 肥胖的
died 死	dad 爸爸	mine 我的	man 男人
bike 自行車	back 背	like 喜歡	lack 缺少

2. 朗讀下列短語及句子，注意雙元音/aɪ/的發音。

like to eat rice 愛吃米飯
try the French fries 嘗嘗炸薯條
like flying in the sky 就像在空中飛
like to ride a bike 喜歡騎自行車
Five times five is twenty-rive.
五五二十五。
Strike while the iron is hot.
趁熱打鐵（英諺）。
Time and tide wait for no man.
歲月不待人（英諺）。
A stitch in time saves nine.
及時處理，事半功倍（英諺）。
Great minds think alike.
英雄所見略同（英諺）。

arrive at five 五點到達
my wife Irene 我妻子艾琳
fly the white kite 放白色的風箏
high time to light the fire 到點火的時間了

3. 朗讀下列小詩。

My kite is white,
My kite is light.
My kite is in the sky!
Now low, now high,
You see my kite,
You see it, you and I.

All day long the sun shines bright,
The moon and the stars come out at night.
From twilight time they line the skies,
And watch the world with quiet eyes.

四、/aʊ/

/aʊ/的發音要領如圖 2-21 所示：

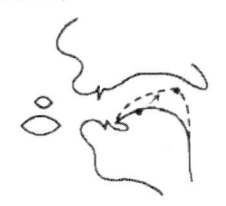

圖 2-21　雙元音/aʊ/

發雙元音/aʊ/時由舌位低、口形大的前元音/a/（此音只在雙元音/aɪ/、/aʊ/中使用）向舌位高、口形小的/ʊ/滑動。結束時的口形是合圓唇，雙唇須稍向前突出。但要注意不可將第二個音發成/uː/。

（一）Words 單詞

a cow　　　　　a blouse
a mouse　　　　a towel
a house　　　　an accountant

（二）Questions and Answers 問答

（1）What are you doing?
你在幹什麼？
I'm milking the cow.
我在擠牛奶。

（2）What is she doing?
她在幹什麼？
She's killing the mouse.
她在消滅耗子。

（3）What's your mother doing?
你媽媽在幹什麼？
She's washing my towel.
她在給我洗毛巾。

（4）What's your father doing?
你爸爸在做什麼？
He's mending my sister's blouse.
他在縫補我妹妹的襯衣。

（5）What's your brother doing?
你哥哥在幹什麼？

He's cleaning our house.
他在打掃房子。

(三) Dialogue 對話

A：Here we are. This is Mr. Brown's house.
我們到了。這裡就是布朗先生的家。

B：Is Brown in?
布朗在家嗎？

A：No, he's gone out.
不在家。他出去了。

B：Is Howard out, too?
霍華德也出去了嗎？

A：I think he's in. Howard! Howard!
我想他在家。霍華德！霍華德！

B：I'll shout a bit louder. How-ard!
我來大聲點叫。霍華德！

(Suddenly Howard's voice is heard. He's singing.)
(突然傳來了霍華德唱歌的聲音。)

A：Yes. I can hear the sound.
是的，我能聽到他的聲音。

B：Yes, he sings loudly.
是啊！他唱歌聲音真大。

A：Well, he sounds like he's shouting.
嗯。他聽起來好像在喊叫（不是唱歌）！

(四) New Words and Expressions 生詞和短語

1. 單詞朗讀：

cow/kaʊ/母牛	mouse/maʊs/老鼠
house/haʊs/房屋，住宅	blouse/blaʊz/女襯衣
towel/ˈtaʊəl, taʊl/毛巾	accountant/əˈkaʊntənt/會計師
milk/mɪlk/牛奶，擠牛奶	kill/kɪl/殺死，弄死
wash/wɒʃ/洗	mend/mend/修理，縫補
clean/kliːn/打掃，使乾淨	our/ˈaʊə/我們的
here/hɪə/這裡	out/aʊt/不在家，外出
shout/ʃaʊt/喊，叫	bit/bɪt/一些，一點
loud/laʊd/大聲的	louder/ˈlaʊdə/（比較級）更大聲的
suddenly/ˈsʌdənlɪ/突然	voice/vɔɪs/（人）聲音，嗓音
sound/saʊnd/聲音	hear/hɪə/聽
sing/sɪŋ/唱歌	

2. 短語朗讀：

| Here we are. 我們到了。 | a bit... 一點…… |

練習

1. 朗讀下列單詞，注意雙元音/aʊ/和單元音/ɒ/之間的區別。

/aʊ/	/ɒ/	/aʊ/	/ɒ/
shout 喊叫	shot 射擊	Brown's 布朗的	bronze 銅
doubt 懷疑	dot 點	spout 壺嘴	spot 地點
pound 英鎊	pond 池子	found 發現	fond 喜愛
scouts 偵察兵	Scots 蘇格蘭人	town 城鎮	Tom 湯姆

2. 朗讀下列短語和句子，注意雙元音/aʊ/的正確發音。

downtown 城區鬧市
bow down 鞠躬
around the house 房子的周圍
down south 南下
Open your mouth and round your lips.
張口圓唇。
Round and round the house shouted the crowd.
人群繞著房子喊叫。
Brown spends hour after hour among his flowers.
布朗在花叢中可以廢寢忘食。
March wind and April showers bring May flowers.
三月的風，四月的雨，迎來五月的花。

a brown tower house 一座棕色塔樓房
found a cow 找到一頭奶牛
around the fountain 繞著噴泉
shouted the scouts 偵察兵喊叫著

3. 朗讀下列小詩，注意雙元音/aʊ/的正確發音。

Cow, cow,
Proud and brown,
Come down to be milked,
For the hungry town.

The owl looked down with his great round eyes.
At the low clouds and the dark skies.
「A good night for scouting,」 says he,
「With never a sound I'll go prowling around.」

第五節 雙元音（2）：集中雙元音

雙元音/ɪə/、/eə/、/ʊə/的發音方式相同：由前一個單音/ɪ/、/e/、/ʊ/向后一個單音/ə/滑動，因而統稱集中雙元音。發音時注意前重后輕、前長后短。

一、/ɪə/

（一）/ɪə/的發音要領
/ɪə/的發音要領如圖 2-22 所示：

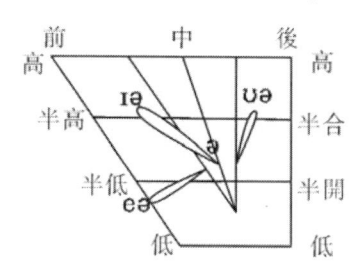

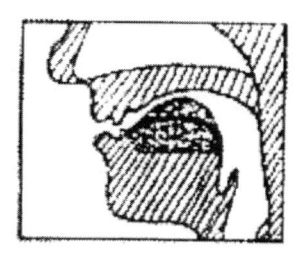

圖 2-22　雙元音/ɪə/

舌位：由舌位較高的前元音/ɪ/向舌位較低的中元音/ə/滑動。
口型：口型扁平，雙唇始終半開。
綜述：/ɪə/是集中雙元音。發音時由/ɪ/音滑向/ə/音。前面的/ɪ/音發得較清楚，后面的/ə/音發得較弱。雙唇始終半開。此音一定要發足。

（二）/ɪə/的發音組合
1. 字母 e 在單詞中常常讀作/ɪə/。
　serial　　　serum　　　serious　　　interior
　cafeteria　 criterion　 experience　　mysterious
2. 字母組合 eer 常常讀作/ɪə/。
　cheer　　　beer　　　peer　　　deer　　　sheer
　sneer　　　steer　　　career　　pioneer　　volunteer
3. 字母組合 ear 常常讀作/ɪə/。
　fear　　　beard　　　weary　　　appear　　　spear
4. 字母組合 ea 常常讀作/ɪə/。
　area　　　idea　　　ideal
5. 字母組合 ere 可讀作/ɪə/。
　mere　　　sere　　　severe　　　interfere

（三）/ɪə/的常見發音錯誤辨析
常見錯誤：
（1）短元音長化：idea—/aɪˈdɪːə/
（2）加入其他音：hear—/hɪjə/

原因辨析：

（1）發音過程中口型未滑動或滑動不到位，前面的/ɪ/音發得較長，后面的/ə/發得較強。

（2）發音過程中口型滑動不自然，加入了半元音/j/。

（四）/ɪə/的發音練習

1. 單詞朗讀：

詞首	
ear/ɪə/耳朵	era/ˈɪərə/紀元；年代
詞中	
zero/ˈzɪərəʊ/零	hero/ˈhɪərəʊ/英雄，豪杰
period/ˈpɪərɪəd/時期，時代	exterior/eksˈtɪərɪə/外面的，外部的
bacteria/bækˈtɪərɪə/細菌	material/məˈtɪərɪəl/物質；原料
inferior/ɪnˈfɪərɪə/下等的	superior/sjuːˈpɪərɪə/上等的
theatre/ˈθɪərɪə/劇場，戲院	realistic/rɪəˈlɪstɪk/現實主義（者）的
詞尾	
dear/dɪə/親愛的；昂貴的	year/jɜː, jɪə/年，歲
near/nɪə/接近，近	hear/hɪə/聽見
shear/ʃɪə/（修）剪，剪羊毛	smear/smɪə/塗，抹
rear/rɪə/撫養；后面的	sincere/sɪnˈsɪə/真摯的
here/hɪə/這裡，在此處	atmosphere/ˈætməsfɪə/大氣（層）；氣氛
tear/tɪə/眼淚，露珠，水珠	clear/klɪə/清澈的；晴朗的；清楚的

2. 短語朗讀：

my dearest 我最親愛的	be all ears 全神貫註地聽
shed no tears 莫要流淚	a fearful liar 大騙子
stand at the rear 站在后邊	here and there 到處
fear nothing 無所畏懼	smear your reputation 玷污你的名譽
shear the sheep 剪羊毛	a sheer fraud 徹頭徹尾的騙局

3. 句子朗讀：

We are near the end of the year.
快到年末了。
His beard has nearly disappeared into his beer.
他的胡子都被啤酒沫蓋住了。
Is there a post-office near here?
附近有郵局嗎？
Things are clear and you don't need to fear.
事情都清楚了，你不必害怕了。
She is all ears and hearing you clearly.
她在聚精會神地聽你講，聽得很清楚。

(五) 欣賞

1. 繞口令：

| Real weird rear wheels. |
| The end of the pier is near, I fear, and the mist hasn't cleared. |
| I see clearly an idea struck him and threw him into great fear. |

2. 諺語：

| Walls have ear.
隔牆有耳。 |
| Hear all parties.
兼聽則明。 |
| Truth never fears investigation.
事實從來不怕調查。 |
| Life is not all beer and skittles.
人生並不全是吃喝玩樂。 |

3. 童謠：

| Hush-a-bye, baby, 不要吵, 小寶寶,
Daddy is near; 爸爸陪你來睡覺；
Mammy's lady, 媽媽不是男子漢,
And that's very clear. 這件事情你知道。 |
| Christmas comes but once a year, 一年一次聖誕,
And when it comes, it brings good cheer, 聖誕人人喜歡,
A pocketful odd money, and a cellar of beer, 又有酒又有錢,
And a good fat pig to last you all the year. 豬肉夠吃一年。 |

二、/eə/

(一) /eə/的發音要領

/eə/的發音要領如圖 2-23 所示：

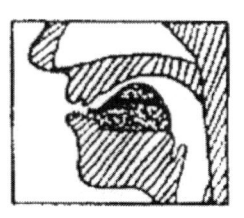

圖 2-23 雙元音 /eə/

發音部位：舌中部。

舌位：發音時舌尖輕觸下齒，前舌略抬起，舌位高度在/e/和/æ/之間。

口型：雙唇半開，口型由中等開合狀滑動至扁平狀。

綜述：/eə/是集中雙元音。發音時從/e/音滑向/ə/音。發音時舌尖抵下齒，前舌略抬起，雙唇半開，此音中的/e/略寬，舌位高度在/e/和/æ/之間。/ə/音較低。

(二) /eə/的發音組合

1. 字母組合 are 常常讀作/eə/。

| care | dare | share | stare | scare |
| bare | flare | hare | rare | affair |

2. 字母組合 air 常常讀作/eə/。

| pair | stair | chair | glair | repair |
| fair | flair | hair | Blair | lair |

3. 字母組合 ere 常常讀作/eə/。

| where | there | nowhere | anywhere | somewhere |

4. 字母組合 ear 常常讀作/eə/。

| wear | bear | tear | pear | swear |

5. 字母 a 在單詞中有時讀作/eə/。

| vary | caries | daring | various | variable |

6. 字母組合 eir 偶爾讀作/eə/。

| Eire | heir | their |

(三) /eə/的常見發音錯誤辨析

常見錯誤：

(1) 窄口型寬大化：where—/waə/

(2) 加入其他音：hair—/heɪe/

原因辨析：

(1) 口型、舌位錯誤。

(2) 滑動不夠快，滑動過程中舌位變高。

(四) /eə/的發音練習

1. 單詞朗讀：

詞首	
air/eə/空氣	area/ˈeərɪə/空地，地面
airway/ˈeəweɪ/航空運輸線	airport/ˈeəpɔːt/航空站
airstrip/ˈeəstrɪp/簡易機場	airtight/ˈeətaɪt/不透氣的；氣密的
airship/ˈeəʃɪp/飛艇	airspace/ˈeəspeɪs/空間；領空
airhostess/ˈeəhəʊstɪs/女乘務員	air-to-air /ˈeə.teə/ 空對空的

詞中	
raring/ˈreərɪŋ/充滿熱情的 varied/ˈveərɪd/各種各樣的 careless/ˈkeəlɪs/粗心的 bareback/ˈbeəbæk/無鞍的 variant/ˈveərɪənt/不同的	rarity/ˈreərɪtɪ/奇事，珍品 careful/ˈkeəfʊl/小心謹慎的 rarefied/ˈreərɪˌfaɪd/稀薄的 farewell/ˌfeəˈwel/再見 variation/ˌveərɪˈeɪʃən/變化
詞尾	
square/skweə/正方形；廣場 prepare/prɪˈpeə/預備，布置 glare/gleə/瞪眼 software/ˈsɒftweə/軟件 despair/dɪsˈpeə/絕望，失望	fare/feə/票價；費 nightmare/ˈnaɪtmeə(r)/夢魘，噩夢 spare/speə/節約，吝惜 repair/rɪˈpeə/修理

2. 短語朗讀：

dare to say 敢說
the lion's share 最大的份額
not turn a hair 不動聲色
eat a lot of pears 吃很多梨
the mare and the hare 母馬和野兔

care to come 想來
run barefoot 赤腳奔跑
a rare metal 稀有金屬
at the trade fair 在交易會上
out of repair 失修

3. 句子朗讀：

I dare not say he is not fair and square.
我不敢說他辦事不公正。
There're some pears on the chair downstairs.
樓下椅子上有些梨。
Mary stares carefully at the huge hairy bear.
瑪麗小心地盯著那頭巨大的多毛熊。
Take good care of the hare, it is very rare.
看護好那只野兔，它非常珍貴。

（五）欣賞

1. 繞口令：

Please prepare the paired pared pears near the unprepared pears near the pool.

That's a rare pair for a mayor to wear and hard to bear as he sits in his chair.

> Beware! That is a bear lair.
> I would not go in there on a dare.
> In there is where a bear scared Pierre.
> Pierre was not aware of the bear in the lair
> Until the bear gave a glare and Pierre ran from there.

2. 諺語：

> Where there's a will, there's a way.
> 有志者事竟成。

> While there is life, there is hope.
> 有生命就有希望。/留得青山在，不怕沒柴燒。

> Constant dropping wears the stone.
> 滴水石穿。

3、歌曲片斷：

> **I SWEAR**
> I see the questions in your eyes.
> I know what's weighing on your mind.
> You can be sure I know my heart.
> Cause I stand beside you through the years.
> You'll only cry those happy tears.
> And though I make mistakes,
> I'll never break your heart.
> I swear by the moon and the stars in the sky... I'll be there.
> I swear like the shadow that's by your side... I'll be there.

三、/ʊə/

（一）/ʊə/的發音要領

/ʊə/的發音要領如圖 2-24 所示：

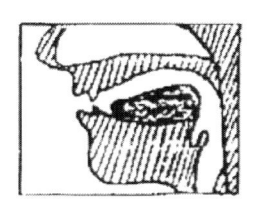

圖 2-24　雙元音/ʊə/

發音部位：舌后部。
舌位：舌后部抬得較高。

口型：口要收圓，雙唇稍突出。由/ʊ/滑向中元音/ə/時口型有明顯的變化，由圓唇改為扁唇。

綜述：/ʊə/是集中雙元音。發音時舌后部抬得較高，口要收圓，雙唇稍突出，由/ʊ/滑向中元音/ə/時口型有明顯的變化，由圓唇改為扁唇。

（二）/ʊə/的發音組合

1. 字母 u 在字母 r 前面常常讀作/ʊə/。

| jury | bureau | purify | rural |
| fury | during | plural | Europe |

2. 字母組合 ou 偶爾讀作/ʊə/。

tourist   tourism

3. 字母組合 ure 有時讀作/ʊə/。

pure   cure   sure   lure

（三）/ʊə/的常見發音錯誤辨析

常見錯誤：

（1）短音長化：sure—/ʃuːə/
（2）小音大音化：tour—/tuːə/
（3）母語化：讀成漢語的「屋餓」；poor—/鋪餓/

原因辨析：

（1）口型錯誤：嘴唇前趨及外延過度。
（2）舌位錯誤：不是用舌根做小動作發音，而是用舌前部發的音。
（3）過於依賴母語。

（四）/ʊə/的發音練習

1. 單詞朗讀：

詞中
curio/ˈkjʊərɪəʊ/古董　　　　　　mural/ˈmjʊərəl/牆壁上的
lurid/ˈljʊərɪd/聳人聽聞的　　　　furious/ˈfjʊərɪəs/狂怒的
purify/ˈpjʊərɪfaɪ/使純淨　　　　　purist/ˈpjʊərɪst/力求純化的人
curious/ˈkjʊərɪəs/好奇的　　　　　bureaucracy/bjʊəˈrɒkrəsɪ/官僚主義
curiosity/ˌkjʊərɪˈɒsɪtɪ/好奇心　　　tropism/ˈtrəʊpɪzəm/旅遊；觀光業
詞尾
pure/pjʊə/純的　　　　　　　　cure/kjʊə/藥；治療
lure/ljʊə/誘惑物，誘餌　　　　　tour/tʊə/旅行
secure/sɪˈkjʊə/安全可靠的　　　　mature/məˈtjʊə/成熟的
impure/ɪmˈpjʊə/臟的　　　　　　obscure/əbˈskjʊə/黑暗的；朦朧的

2. 短語朗讀：

make sure 確信	jury member 陪審團成員
mature plans 周密的計劃	curious boy 好奇的男孩
running at a furious pace 疾奔	all series of cures 各種藥物
pure water 淨水	
package tour 由旅行社代辦全部事宜的觀光旅遊	

3. 句子朗讀：

These newer attractions are sure to lure the tourists.
這些新景點肯定能吸引住遊客。
The doctor is sure to be able to cure the poor girl.
醫生一定能醫好這個可憐的姑娘。
The tourists were curious to know the story behind the mural.
遊客們對隱藏在壁畫後面的故事非常好奇。

(五) 欣賞

1. 繞口令：

We surely shall see the sun shine soon.

A lusty lady loved a lawyer and longed to lure him from his laboratory.

「Surely Sylvia swims!」shrieked Sammy, surprised,「Someone should show Sylvia some strokes so she shall not sink.」

2. 諺語：

Prevention is better than cure.
預防勝於治療。

Time cures all things.
時間是醫治一切創傷的良藥。

第三章 輔音

第一節 輔音音標符號及其發音要領

一、爆破音：/p/、/b/、/t/、/d/、/k/、/g/

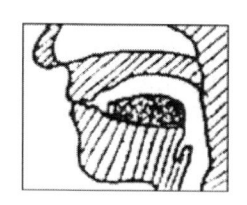

/p/、/b/英式讀音符號
/p/、/b/傳統的國際音標讀音符號
/p/、/b/美式讀音符號

/p/是字母 p 的發音，/b/是字母 b 的讀音。它們是雙唇爆破輔音。發音要領是雙唇緊閉，憋住氣，然后突然分開，氣流衝出口腔，發出爆破音。/p/是清輔音，聲帶不振動；/b/是濁輔音，聲帶振動。

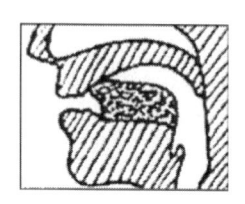

/t/、/d/英式讀音符號
/t/、/d/傳統的國際音標讀音符號
/t/、/d/美式讀音符號

/t/是字母 t 的發音，/d/是字母 d 的讀音。它們是舌齒爆破輔音。發音要領是舌尖抵上齒齦，憋住氣，然后突然分開，使氣流衝出口腔，發出爆破音。/t/是清輔音，聲帶不振動；/d/是濁輔音，聲帶振動。

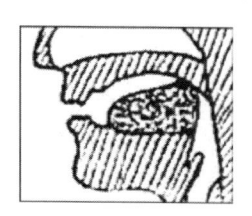

/k/、/g/英式讀音符號

/k/、/g/傳統的國際音標讀音符號

/k/、/g/美式讀音符號

/k/是字母 k 和字母 c 的讀音，/g/是字母 g 的讀音。它們是舌后軟腭爆破輔音。發音要領是舌后部隆起緊貼軟腭，憋住氣，然后突然分開，氣流送出口腔，形成爆破音。/k/是清輔音，聲帶不振動；/g/是濁輔音，聲帶振動。

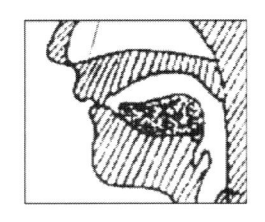

二、摩擦音：/f/、/v/、/θ/、/ð/、/s/、/z/、/ʃ/、/ʒ/、/h/、/r/

/f/、/v/英式讀音符號

/f/、/v/傳統的國際音標讀音符號

/f/、/v/美式讀音符號

/f/是字母 f 和字母組合 ph 的讀音，/v/是字母 v 的讀音。它們是唇齒摩擦輔音。發音要領是下唇輕觸上齒，氣流由唇齒間通過，形成摩擦音。/f/是清輔音，聲帶不振動；/v/是濁輔音，聲帶振動。

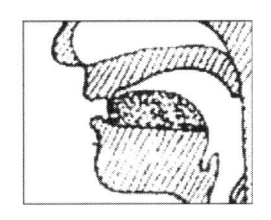

/θ/、/ð/英式讀音符號

/θ/、/ð/傳統的國際音標讀音符號

/θ/、/ð/美式讀音符號

/θ/、/ð/是字母組合 th 的讀音。它們是舌齒摩擦輔音。發音要領是舌尖輕觸上齒背，氣流由舌齒間送出，形成摩擦音。/θ/是清輔音，聲帶不振動；/ð/是濁輔音，聲帶振動。

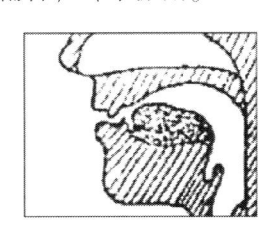

第三章　輔音

85

/s/、/z/英式讀音符號

/s/、/z/傳統的國際音標讀音符號

/s/、/z/美式讀音符號

/s/、/z/是字母 s 的讀音，而/z/又是字母 z 的讀音。它們是舌齒摩擦輔音。發音要領是舌端靠近齒齦，氣流由舌端齒齦間送出，形成摩擦音。/s/是清輔音，聲帶不振動；/z/是濁輔音，聲帶振動。

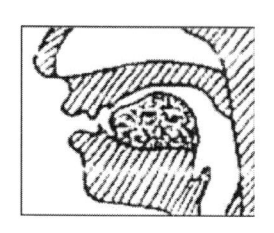

/ʃ/、/ʒ/英式讀音符號

/ʃ/、/ʒ/傳統的國際音標讀音符號

/ʃ/、/ʒ/美式讀音符號

/ʃ/是字母組合 sh 的讀音，/ʒ/是字母 s 的讀音。它們是舌端齒齦后部摩擦輔音。發音要領是舌端靠近齒齦后部，舌身抬起靠近上腭，雙唇稍收圓並略突出，氣流通過時形成摩擦音。/ʃ/是清輔音，聲帶不振動；/ʒ/是濁輔音，聲帶振動。

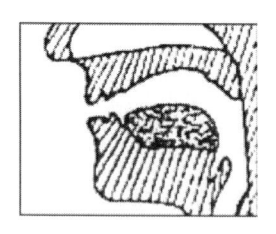

/h/英式讀音符號

/h/傳統的國際音標讀音符號

/h/美式讀音符號

/h/是字母 h 的讀音。它是聲門摩擦輔音。發音要領是氣流送出口腔，在通過聲門時發出輕微摩擦；口形隨其后的元音而變化。/h/是清輔音，聲帶不振動。

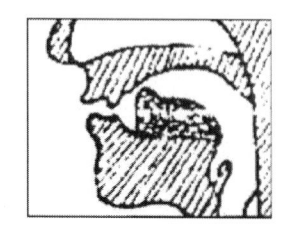

/r/英式讀音符號

/r/傳統的國際音標讀音符號

/r/美式讀音符號

/r/是字母 r 的讀音。它是舌尖齒齦（后部）摩擦輔音。發音要領是舌尖卷起，靠近上齒齦后部，舌兩側稍收攏，雙唇略突出，氣流通過舌尖和齒齦形成輕微摩擦。/r/是濁輔音，聲帶振動。

三、破擦音：/tʃ/、/dʒ/、/ts/、/dz/、/tr/、/dr/

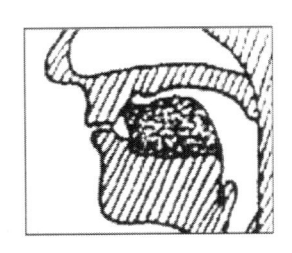

/tʃ/、/dʒ/英式讀音符號

/tʃ/、/dʒ/傳統的國際音標讀音符號

/tʃ/、/dʒ/美式讀音符號

/tʃ/是字母組合 ch 的讀音，/dʒ/是字母組合 dge 的讀音。它們是舌端齒齦破擦輔音。發音要領是舌身抬高，舌端抵上齒齦后部，氣流通過時發出破擦音。/tʃ/是清輔音，聲帶不振動；/dʒ/是濁輔音，聲帶振動。

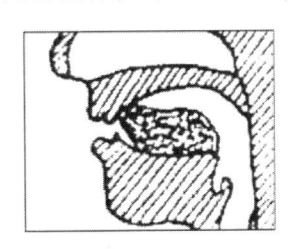

/ts/、/dz/英式讀音符號

/ts/、/dz/傳統的國際音標讀音符號

/ts/、/dz/美式讀音符號

/ts/是字母組合 ts 的讀音，/dz/是字母組合 ds 的讀音。它們是舌端齒齦破擦輔音。發音要領是舌端先貼住齒齦，堵住氣流，然后略下降，將氣流送出口腔。/ts/是清輔音，/dz/是濁輔音。

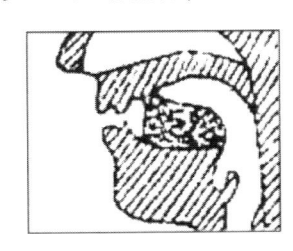

/tr/、/dr/英式讀音符號

第三章　輔音

87

/tr/、/dr/傳統的國際音標讀音符號

/tr/、/dr/美式讀音符號

　　/tr/是字母組合 tr 的讀音，/dr/是字母組合 dr 的讀音。它們是齒齦后部破擦輔音。發音要領是舌身與/r/相似，舌尖貼齒齦后部，氣流衝破阻礙發出短促的/t/后立即發/r/。/tr/是清輔音，/dr/是濁輔音。

　　四、鼻音：/m/、/n/、/ŋ/

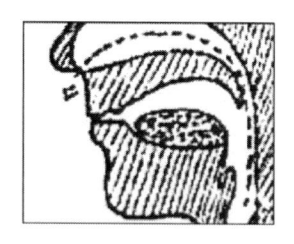

/m/英式讀音符號

/m/傳統的國際音標讀音符號

/m/美式讀音符號

　　/m/是字母 m 的讀音。它是雙唇鼻輔音。發音要領是軟腭下垂，雙唇緊閉，氣流從鼻腔送出。

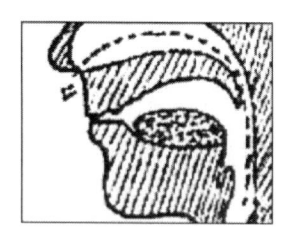

/n/英式讀音符號

/n/傳統的國際音標讀音符號

/n/美式讀音符號

　　/n/是字母 n 的讀音。它是舌尖齒齦鼻輔音。發音要領是舌尖抵上齒齦，軟腭下垂，氣流從鼻腔送出。

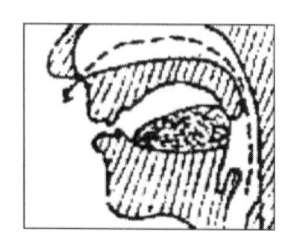

/ŋ/英式讀音符號

/ŋ/傳統的國際音標讀音符號

/ŋ/美式讀音符號

/ŋ/是字母組合 ng 的讀音。它是舌后軟腭鼻輔音。發音要領是軟腭下垂，堵住口腔通道，氣流從鼻腔送出，聲帶振動。

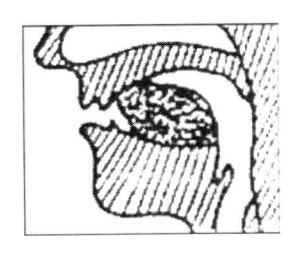

五、舌側音：/l/

/l/英式讀音符號
/l/傳統的國際音標讀音符號
/l/美式讀音符號

/l/是字母 l 的讀音。它是舌端齒齦邊輔音。發音要領是舌尖及舌端緊貼上齒齦，舌前向硬腭抬起，氣流從舌的旁邊送出；當此音為尾音時，將舌端抵住上齒齦，舌前下陷，舌后上抬，舌面形成凹形。/l/是濁輔音，發音時聲帶振動。

第二節　輔音字母的發音

英語中輔音字母在單詞中的發音是怎樣的？輔音字母組合的發音有哪些規律？像 great 中的/gr/這樣的輔音連綴到底該怎樣發音才準確呢？這些就是我們在本節中將要共同學習的內容。

一、輔音字母的發音

英語中共有 21 個輔音字母。那麼這 21 個輔音字母在單詞中的發音規律是怎樣的呢？讓我們一起來看一下表 3-1。

表 3-1　　　　　　　　21 個輔音字母發音規律表

輔音字母	讀音	輔音字母所在位置	例詞
b	/b/	一般情況	big, bad, blue, pub, tube
	不發音	在 m 后或在 t 前	climb, comb, lamb, doubt, debt
c	/k/	一般情況	cake, cap, coffee, cold, cup, culture, class
	/s/	在 e, i, y 前	cell, century, rice, city, cigarette, Lucy, juicy
	/ʃ/	在 ia, ie, io 前	social, especial, ancient, appreciate, beneficial

89

表3-1(續1)

輔音字母	讀音	輔音字母所在位置	例詞
d	/d/	一般情況	desk, dad, dog, good, grade
	不發音	在-dge中	edge, bridge
f	/f/	一般情況	flag, floor, food, few, leaf, half, self
	/v/	個別特例	of
g	/g/	一般情況	give, girl, glass, green, glad, agree, pig, dog
	/dʒ/	在 e, i, y 前或在-dge中	large, orange, logic, gym, energy, judge
	不發音	在以 gn 結尾的詞中	sign, design, foreign
h	/h/	一般情況	have, head, help, hat, home, here, health, heaven
	不發音	在個別詞中	honest, hour, honor, John, when, where, oh
j	/dʒ/	一般無特例	joke, jacket, jet, jeep, jam, jar
k	/k/	一般情況	Kate, kick, key, kite, talk, smoke, joke
	不發音	在字母 n 前	know, knee, knock, knife, know
l	/l/	一般情況	leg, let, left, loss, apple, told
	不發音	在-alf,-alm,-alk,-ould 中	half, calm, alarm, talk, chalk, could, should
m	/m/	一般無特例	me, man, meet, meal, map, mouth
n	/n/	一般情況	new, nod, nine, nice, line, fine
	/ŋ/	在字母 k, g 或/k/音前	anxious, think, thank, blank, bank, finger, uncle
p	/p/	一般無特例	map, jeep, pig, pen, apple, camp
q	/kw/	在 qu-中	quick, quit, question, quarter
	/k/	單獨出現	Iraq
r	/r/	一般無特例	red, read, rabbit
s	/s/	詞首	sun, sad, save, sand, smell, start, still
	/z/	元音字母和元音字母之間	visit, season, prison, desire, music, represent
	/s/	元音字母和不發音的e之間	house, case, close (名詞或形容詞中)
	/z/		close, raise (動詞中)
	/s/	詞中清輔音前	past, guest, desk, task grasp, newspaper
	/z/	詞中濁輔音前	husband, salesgirl, newsreel
	/ʃ/	非重讀音節中在-ia 或-io 前(前為輔音),重讀音節 su 中,非重讀音節的詞尾-sure 中(前為輔音)	sure, Asia, Russia, discussion, pressure, sugar
	/ʒ/	非重讀音節中在-ia 或-io 之前(前為元音),非重讀音節的詞尾-sure 中(前為元音)	pleasure, usually, occasion, television, decision

表3-1(續2)

輔音字母	讀音	輔音字母所在位置	例詞
t	/t/	一般情況	sit, tea, west, guest, table, little
	/ʃ/	在 ia, ie, io 前	nation, patient, partial
	不發音	在 -sten, -stle, -ften 中	listen, often, soften, castle, whistle
	/tʃ/	在 -ture, -tural 中	future, culture, natural
v	/v/	一般無特例	five, vase, very, seven, victory, glove
w	/w/	一般情況	we, window, watch, want, wide, sweet
	不發音	在字母 r 前或在字母 s 后	write, wrap, wrong, wrist, answer, sword
x	/ks/	一般情況	exercise, excuse, except, fix, box, taxi
	/gz/	元音字母前	exam, exit, example, exactly, exert
y	/j/	詞首	yes, yell, yellow, yet, young
	/aɪ/	重讀音節的詞尾	fly, cry, why, by, my
	/ɪ/	非重讀音節的詞尾	happy, city, baby, family
z	/z/	一般無特例	zoo, zero, zebra, zigzag, biz, puzzle

二、輔音字母組合的發音

英語中，輔音字母組合是很常見的，也是非常豐富的，如 ch, dr, th, tr, sh, wr, gh, gn, ng, ph, tch, tion, sion, ture 等。

其中大部分的發音是唯一的。例如：dr 總是發成 /dr/，ph 總是發成 /f/，tch 總是發成 /tʃ/，wr 總是發成 /r/。

還有一些輔音字母組合的發音與其在單詞中相鄰的音節有關。例如：字母組合 wh 通常發成 /w/，如在單詞 what, why 和 white 中；而當 wh 組合出現在字母 o 的前面時，就要發成 /h/ 了，如在單詞 who, whom 和 whole 中。

另外一些輔音字母組合的發音與其在單詞中所處的位置有關。例如：gn 出現在詞首或詞尾一般發成 /n/，如在單詞 foreign 和 gnat 中；而出現在詞中的時候要發成 /gn/，如 designation, signature。

更多更詳細的輔音字母組合發音規律請看表 3-2 中的總結。

表 3-2　　　　　　　　輔音字母組合發音規律表

輔音字母組合	位置	讀音	例詞
ch		/tʃ/	child, chair, chicken, catch, watch
		/k/	school, chemistry, Christmas, stomachache
		/ʃ/	chef, Chicago, machine, moustache
ck		/k/	pick, quick, back, kick, pack, black

表3-2(續)

輔音字母組合	位置	讀音	例詞
dr		/dr/	dream, dress, drive, draw, hundred
ds		/dz/	birds, hands, beds, friends, cards
gh		/f/	enough, cough, laugh, tough, rough
gn	詞首或詞尾	/n/	foreign, design, resign, reign, gnat
gn	詞中	/gn/	designation, signature
gu		/gw/	language
kn		/n/	know, knock, knife, knee, knit, knowledge
mb		/m/	numb, thumb, limb
mn		/m/	autumn, column, solemn
ng		/ŋ/	sing, ring, something, nothing
ng		/ŋg/	hungry, language, English
nk		/ŋk/	thank, think, blank, wink, frankly
ph		/f/	phone, photo, phrase, physics, telegraph
qu		/kw/	quick, quiet, question, quarter, earthquake
sh		/ʃ/	short, fish, English, share, show, flash
th		/θ/	think, thing, throw, mouth, growth
th		/ð/	this, that, these, those, there, with, though
tch		/tʃ/	match, catch, fetch, patch
tr		/tr/	tree, train, trade, traffic, trousers, trouble
ts, tes	詞尾	/ts/	cats, jackets, sweets, kites
tw		/tw/	twelve, twice, twin, twist
wr		/r/	wrong, wrist, wretch, wrap
wh	在字母 o 前	/h/	who, whom, whose, whole
wh	一般情況	/w/	what, why, where, wheel, white, whisky
tion	一般情況	/ʃən/	education, direction, station, situation
tion	在字母 s 前	/tʃən/	suggestion, question
sion	元音字母後	/ɛən/	decision, conclusion, television
sion	其他字母後	/ʃən/	permission, expression, mission
tle	詞尾	/tl/	bottle, cattle, little, gentle
ture	詞尾	/tʃə/	picture, gesture, culture, nature

三、輔音連綴

你聽說過英語中的輔音連綴現象嗎？在同一意群內，如果有兩個或兩個以上

的輔音音素結合在一起，這種語音現象就是輔音連綴。

輔音連綴不僅可能出現在詞首，也都有可能出現在詞中和詞尾。常見的出現在詞首和詞中的輔音連綴，如/sp/、/st/、/sf/、/sm/、/sn/、/sl/、/sw/、/pl/、/tr/、/kl/、/bl/、/dr/、/gl/、/fl/、/θr/、/spr/、/str/、/skr/、/spl/、/skw/等。再如出現在詞尾的常見輔音連綴/rk/、/rg/、/rp/、/rt/、/rd/、/lk/、/lp/、/lt/、/nt/、/nd/、/ns/、/nz/等。一般來說，元音前連綴的輔音不會超過3個，元音后連綴的輔音不會超過4個。

有些英語學習者習慣性地在各個輔音之間加入某個元音，其中/ə/最為常見。例如一定有學習者在 great /greɪt/的/g/和/r/中間加入了一個元音/ə/而錯讀成了/gəreɪt/，比較常見的再如有些同學習慣把 cream /kriːm/錯讀成/kəriːm/，還有一些學習者總是將輔音之間的連接過渡讀得不連貫也不自然，這些都是在英語學習中特別應該注意改正的地方。

以下是一些在詞首或詞中經常出現的輔音連綴結構及其例詞：

/sk/	sky, ski, skill, skate, skeleton
/sp/	spy, spring, Spain, speak, spot
/st/	stay, star, start, stage, staff
/sf/	sphere, transfer
/sm/	smell, small, smart, smash, smoke
/sn/	snow, snake, snack, sneeze, sneer
/kj/	cute, cucumber, cure, curious, curiosity
/skj/	skewer, skew
/bj/	beautiful, bureau
/pj/	pure, purify, pupil, deputy, dispute
/spj/	spurious, spume
/dj/	due, duty, dubious, dude, duration
/tj/	Tuesday, tune, tube, tutor, tuition
/stj/	student, studious, stupid, studio
/vj/	view, Vietnam
/fj/	few, fuel, funeral, futile, nephew
/sj/	sue, super, suitcase, suicide
/hj/	huge, human, humor, humid, humiliate
/mj/	music, amusement, museum, mutual, mute
/nj/	new, nuclear, nutrition, avenue
/gl/	glad, glass, glove, global, glorious
/kl/	club, close, clean, clause, classroom
/bl/	black, blue, blow, bloom, blank

/pl/	plan, please, place, plane, planet
/spl/	split, splendid, splice, splash
/fl/	fly, flee, float, flesh, flower
/sl/	sleep, slow, slide, slot, slogan
/gr/	grow, grey, green, great, graduate
/kr/	cry, crazy, crop, create, microphone
/skr/	screen, scream, describe, skyscraper, transcript
/br/	brand, bring, brain, broad, February
/pr/	pride, present, praise, pretty, practice
/spr/	spring, sprite
/dr/	dream, draw, drink, dragon, hundred
/tr/	tree, train, traffic, country, control
/str/	string, street, straight, strategy, strawberry
/fr/	frozen, France, fresh, Friday
/θr/	three, throw, through, threat, threshold
/ʃr/	shrimp, shrink, shred, shrug, mushroom
/gw/	Gwadar, Gwen
/kw/	quite, quick, question, quality, quarter
/skw/	square, squirrel, squad, squeeze
/dw/	dwell, dwarf
/tw/	twin, twice, twelve, twenty, twist
/θw/	thwart
/sw/	sweet, swim, swallow, swear, sweater

下面是一些詞尾常見的輔音連綴結構及其例詞：

/rk/	bark, dark, park, shark, ark
/kg/	morgue
/rp/	sharp
/rb/	barb
/rt/	art, fart, dart, fort, sort
/rd/	hard, lord, ford, word
/rtʃ/	church, March
/rdʒ/	large, merge, submerge, serge
/rf/	scarf
/rv/	carve, harvest
/rθ/	north, worth, birth, earth
/rs/	horse, course, source

/rz/	Mars
/rʃ/	harsh, marsh
/rm/	farm, firm, form, transform, worm
/rn/	born, corn, warn, scorn, worn
/rl/	girl, whirl, world
/lk/	milk, silk
/lp/	help
/lb/	bulb
/lt/	belt, felt, delta, wilt, consult
/ld/	old, elder, bald, hold, fold
/ltʃ/	Welch
/ldʒ/	bulge
/lf/	elf, self, shelf, wolf
/lv/	solve, involve, Volvo
/lθ/	health, wealth
/ls/	else, false
/lʃ/	Welsh
/lm/	film
/ln/	kiln
/ŋk/	ink, think, thank, blank, monk
/mp/	jump, camp, glimpse, pumpkin
/nt/	aunt, ant, faint, paint, joint
/nd/	and, find, second, behind, hand
/ntʃ/	lunch, branch, inch
/ndʒ/	change
/mf/	triumph
/nθ/	month
/ns/	dance
/nz/	Benz, fans
/kt/	act, fact, conduct, product, shocked
/ŋkt/	extinct, linked
/pt/	adopt, adapt
/mpt/	attempt, contempt, prompts
/ks/	six, fix, mix, cakes, Marks
/ŋks/	jinx
/ps/	collapse
/mps/	glimpse, jumps

第三章　輔音

/sk/	desk, task, disk
/sp/	grasp, wasp, aspiration
/st/	fast, gist, haste
/nst/	against
/ts/	blitz
/rts/	quartz
/lts/	waltz
/ft/	lift, shift, left, handcraft

練習

1. 請試著列舉一些含有輔音連綴的詞彙。

2. 請給下面單詞中的字母 s 或者 ss 標上音標。

silk（　）　　television（　）　　raise（　）　　close（　）
sugar（　）　　Russia（　）　　　discussion（　）　decision（　）
case（　）　　represent（　）　　salesgirl（　）　measure（　）
visit（　）　　usually（　）　　　buses（　）　　newspaper（　）
desire（　）　　guest（　）　　　pressure（　）　closure（　）
listen（　）　　pleasure（　）　　stand（　）　　occasion（　）
question（　）　stand（　）　　　biscuit（　）　　impression（　）
famous（　）　vision（　）　　　these（　）　　suggestion（　）

3. 下列單詞中的字母 g 都發音嗎？請標出單詞中不發音的字母 g。

foreign　　　language　　　great　　　gnat　　　enough
designation　goose　　　　sign　　　ring　　　English
something　　caught　　　　glad　　　ghost　　logic
game　　　　diagnosis　　　large　　　grade　　resign
grass　　　　straight　　　campaign　judge　　weight
hungry　　　glue　　　　　gym　　　thought　paradigm
design　　　orange　　　　Greece　　high　　　gnash
grow　　　　energetic　　　signature　caught　gene

4. 朗讀下列繞口令，在讀對讀準的基礎上嘗試漸漸加快速度，看看你的口齒夠伶俐嗎？請特別注意輔音字母及輔音字母組合的發音。

（1）I scream, you scream, we all scream for ice-cream!

（2）The best lest in the West is the Vest Fest.

（3）A big black bug bit a big black dog on his big black nose!

（4）Tom's got a lot of dots on his pocket. If he wants to wash off the dots, he will use a pot of hot water.

（5）I'm very wary of very scary films.

（6）Good cookies could be cooked by a good cook, if a good cook could cook good cookies.

（7）Three thin thieves thought a thousand thoughts.

Now if three thin thieves thought a thousand thoughts,

How many thoughts did each thief think?

（8）Peter Piper picked a peck of pickle prepared by his parents and put them in a big paper plate.

（9）Whether the weather be fine or whether the weather be not,

Whether the weather be cold or whether the weather be hot,

We'll weather the weather whether we like it or not.

（10）How many sheets could a sheet slitter slit if a sheet slitter could slit sheets?

5. 朗讀下面幾則小笑話，注意其中輔音字母的發音。

Who Is More Polite?

A fat man and a skinny man were arguing about who was more polite.

The skinny man said he was more polite because he always tipped his hat to ladies. But the fat man knew he was more courteous because whenever he got up and offered his seat, two ladies could sit down.

More Intelligent in Dreams

When a student failed to solve a math problem in class, he expressed his regret to his teacher, 「I remember solving the problem in my dream last night, but for the time being I've forgotten it. What can that mean?」

「It means that you are more intelligent in dreams than when you are awake,」 the teacher explained.

A Special Crab

A male crab met a female crab and asked her to marry him. She noticed that he was walking straight instead of sideways. Wow, she thought, this crab is really special. I can't let him get away. So they got married immediately.

The next day she noticed her new husband walking sideways like all the other crabs, and got up set, 「What happened?」 she asked, 「You used to walk straight before we were married.」

「Oh, honey,」 he replied, 「I can't drink that much every day.」

第四章 音節

第一節 音節

　　音節是讀音的基本單位，任何單詞的讀音，都可以分解為一個個的音節來讀。在英語中元音特別響亮，一個元音音素可構成一個音節，一個元音音素和一個或幾個輔音音素結合也可以構成一個音節。一般說來，元音音素可以構成音節，輔音音素不響亮，不能構成音節。但英語輔音音素中的/m/、/n/、/ŋ/、/l/和其他某些輔音音素結合，也可構成音節。它們構成的音節常出現在詞尾，一般是非重讀音節。

　　英語單詞讀音有一個音節的、兩個音節的和多個音節的。一個音節的單詞叫單音節詞，兩個音節的單詞叫雙音節詞，三個音節及以上的單詞叫多音節詞。

　　每個元音音素都可以構成一個音節。元音構成音節的中心，稱為音節峰（Peak），音節峰前面的輔音為音節首（Onset），其后面的輔音為音節尾（Coda），如 bed 一詞的音標為/bed/，其中/e/為音節峰，/b/為音節首，/d/為音節尾。兩個元音音素也可以構成一個音節，如 jeep /dʒiːp/中的/dʒ/為音節首，/iː/為音節峰，/p/為音節尾。

一、重讀音節與非重讀音節

　　重讀音節指在雙音節或多音節詞中那個發音特別響亮的音節，用重音符號「ˈ」標於相應位置，其他音節為非重讀音節，如 begin/bɪˈɡɪn/，astound /əˈstaʊnd/，ostrich/ˈɔstrɪtʃ/。單音節詞朗讀時作重讀處理，但不標重音符號。

　　重讀音節以外的音節為非重讀音節。一般單詞中有超過一個音節時就有重讀音節和非重讀音節的區別。如在單詞 lazy/ˈleɪzi/中，第一個音節為重讀音節，第二個音節則為非重讀音節。超過兩個音節的單詞中有時會有重讀音節、次重讀音節和非重讀音節之分。如 examination/ɪɡˌzæmɪˈneɪʃən/中有五個音節，其中第四個音節為重讀音節，第一個音節為次重讀音節，第二、三、五個音節為非重讀音節。

二、音節的組成

　　音節是讀音的基本單位，任何單詞的讀音，都是分解為一個個音節朗讀。在英語中元音特別響亮，一個元音可構成一個音節，一個元音和一個或幾個輔音音素結合也可以構成一個音節。

常見的形式有：

（1）元音，如：i—/aɪ/、a—/eɪ/等；

（2）輔音+元音，如：she—/ʃiː/、bee—/biː/、me—/miː/等；

（3）元音+輔音，如：egg—/eg/、ink—/ɪŋk/、am—/æm, əm/等；

（4）輔音+元音+輔音，如：pig—/pɪg/、big—/bɪg/、leg—/leg/、swim—/swɪm/等。

此外英語裡還有一種特殊音節，其構成沒有元音的參與。輔音/l/和/n/是成音節輔音，前面加上另一個輔音如：/bl/、/dl/、/tl/、/tn/、/sl/即可構成一個音節，如：table—/ˈteɪbl/、middle—/ˈmɪdl/、bottle—/ˈbɒtl/、rotton—/ˈrɒtn/、pencil—/ˈpensl/等。此為音節構成的第五種方式，即：

（5）輔音+輔音，如：people—/ˈpiːpl/、little—/ˈlɪtl/、parcel—/ˈpɑːsl/等。

三、開音節和閉音節

英語中的開音節可分為絕對開音節和相對開音節：

·絕對開音節：是指一個元音音素后面沒有輔音音素而構成的音節，如 she, he, stay 等。

·相對開音節：是指一個元音音素后面有一個輔音音素（除 r 之外），最后是一個不發音的 e 字母構成的重讀音節，如 late, theme, excuse 等。

在重讀開音節中，這個元音字母發字母本身的音，如 late/leɪt/、she/ʃiː/、like/laɪk/、dote/dəʊt/、duke/djuːk/等。

閉音節指元音字母后面加輔音字母（輔音字母 r, w 和 y 除外）構成的音節，如 pet/pet/、rush/rʌʃ/、mob/mɒb/、start/stɑːt/等。

英語的音節按讀音可以分為開音節和閉音節，開音節又可以分為絕對開音節和相對開音節。

絕對開音節是指在一個音節中，元音字母后面沒有輔音字母而構成的音節。例如：he—/hiː/、be—/biː/、do—/duː/、so—/səʊ/、no—/nəʊ/等。

相對開音節是指在一個音節中，元音字母、后面的一個輔音字母（除 r）和最后的一個不發音的字母 e 構成的音節。例如：lake—/leɪk/、site—/saɪt/、note—/nəʊt/等。

在重讀開音節中，元音字母發「字母」本身讀音，即：a—/eɪ/、e—/iː/、i—/aɪ/、o—/əʊ/、u—/juː/。例如：name—/neɪm/、Kate—/keɪt/、she—/ʃiː/、Chinese—/ˈtʃaɪˈniːz/、bike—/baɪk/、nice—/naɪs/、go—/gəʊ/、hello—/ˈheləʊ, heˈləʊ/、use—/juːs/、duty—/ˈdjuːtɪ/等。

閉音節是指在一個音節中，元音字母和后面的一個或多個輔音字母（輔音字母 r 除外）構成的音節。例如：big—/bɪg/、map—/mæp/、stop—/stɒp/等。

在重讀閉音節中，元音字母發相應的短音，即：a—/æ/、e—/e/、i—/ɪ/、

o—/ɒ/，u—/ʌ/。例如：cat—/kæt/，can—/kæn，kən/，wet—/wet/，next—/nekst/，wit—/wɪt/，miss—/mɪs/，dog—/dɒg/，box—/bɒks/，but—/bət/，cup—/kʌp/等。

四、重讀閉音節

英語重讀閉音節指一個音節以輔音音素結尾而且是重讀音節，如 little 一詞中的第一個音節。重讀閉音節的三要素：①必須是重讀音節；②最後只有一個輔音字母；③元音字母發短元音。

如果因為語法的原因，需要改變詞形，那麼以重讀閉音節結尾的單詞就要雙寫最後一個輔音字母，如 set—setting, begin—beginning, swim—swimming 等。

五、「r」音節

「r」音節指元音字母或元音字母組合后面有一個輔音字母 r 構成的音節，包括：ar, er, ir, or, ur, air, ear, eer, eir, oar, oor, our。例如，下列單詞中就含有「r」音節：party, artist, perfect, servant, skirt, flirt, sport, orphan, purchase, fur, stair, pair, bear, earnest, pioneer, peer, their, heir, roar, boar, floor, poor, flour, pour。

六、音節的劃分

英語的單詞有一個音節的單音節詞，兩個音節的雙音節詞，以及三個音節以上的多音節詞。例如：

單音節詞——a, am, can;
雙音節詞——a/gain, stu/dy, sis/ter, far/mer;
多音節詞——si/tu/a/tion, in/for/ma/tion, ex/pen/sive。

元音是構成音節的主體，輔音是音節的分界線。劃分音節應以它的語音形式，而不是以書寫形式為依據。

（1）兩元音字母之間有一個輔音字母時，輔音字母歸后一音節，如：na/tion, fa/vour, po/si/tion, po/pu/lar。

（2）有兩個輔音字母時，一個輔音字母歸前一音節，一個歸后一音節，如：mem/ber, sis/ter, en/ter, cur/rent。

（3）不能拆分的字母組合，按字母組合劃分音節，如：daugh/ter, fea/ther, lea/der, wea/ther。

開音節要在元音字母后面分開，如 teacher—tea·cher, banana—ba·na·na, student—stu·dent 等。閉音節要從兩個輔音字母之間分開，如 letter—let·ter, kidnap—kid·nap, export—ex·port 等。合成詞要從兩個單詞中間分開，如 classmate—class·mate, warmhouse—warm·house, textbook—text·book 等。混合

情況，如 businessman—bu・si・ness・man，computer—com・pu・ter，important—im・por・tant 等。

練習

1. 請根據本章所學內容，分別舉例列出開音節詞、重讀閉音節詞各 10 個。

2. 根據音節劃分的知識，將下面的單詞劃分音節。

interference	antecedent	engineer	mathematics	inevitability
familiarity	Chinese	thirteen	bourgeoisie	Indiana
Alexander	continuity	magazine	university	exhibition
entertainment	yogurt	interesting	newspaper	

3. 劃分下列單詞的音節，並標出其音標。

but	butter	butterfly
late	later	lately
harm	hardly	harmony
debt	debate	December
push	punish	punishment

4. 劃分下列單詞的音節，注意成音節字母組合的讀音。

| cable | listen | vital | fatal | mutton |
| eagle | jungle | often | basin | burden |

第二節　單詞重音

一、重讀音節和非重讀音節

重讀音節，指在雙音節或多音節詞中有一個發音特別響亮的音節，叫重讀音節，用重音符號「ˈ」標於相應位置。其他音節為非重讀音節。如 ago—/əˈɡəʊ/ 中，/ə/ 為非重讀音節，/ˈɡəʊ/ 為重讀音節。

二、單音節詞、雙音節詞和多音節詞

單音節詞：單音節詞作重讀處理，但不標重音符號。

雙音節詞：在朗讀雙音節詞時，一個音節要重讀，一個音節要輕讀，為了區別輕重就須在重讀音節的左上方打上重音符號。如：latter—/ˈlætə/，sister—/ˈsɪstə/，father—/ˈfɑːðə/。

多音節詞：（三個音節以上的詞）除了重讀音節外，還得加上一個次重讀音

節（即：第二重音）符號，打在該音節的左下方。第二重音比第一重音稍輕些。例如：International—/ˌIntə(ː)ˈnæʃənəl/，manufacture—/ˌmænjʊˈfæktʃə/。

三、重音規則

（一）雙音節詞

雙音節名詞和形容詞的重音常常在第一個音節上。例如：

lucky—/ˈlʌkɪ/，lazy—/ˈleɪzɪ/，mother—/ˈmʌðə/，farmer—/ˈfɑːmə/。

少數雙音節詞的重音也可以落在第二個音節上，一般是外來語，如法語詞。例如：

hotel—/həʊˈtel/，machine—/məˈʃiːn/，police—/pəˈliːs/。

雙音節動詞的重音常常在第二個音節上。例如：

forget—/fəˈget/，propose—/prəˈpəʊz/，advise—/ədˈvaɪz/，suggest—/səˈdʒest/。

名詞、動詞拼法相同的雙音節詞：重音在前是名詞，重音在後是動詞。例如：

名詞——動詞

ˈcontest—conˈtest   ˈcontrast—conˈtrast
export—exˈport   ˈimport—imˈport
ˈincrease—inˈcrease   ˈobject—obˈject
ˈinsult—inˈsult   ˈrecord—reˈcord
ˈsurvey—surˈvey   ˈinput—inˈput

（二）三音節詞

三音節詞的重音一般在第一個音節上。例如：

family—/ˈfæmɪlɪ/   company—/ˈkʌmpənɪ/
summary—/ˈsʌmərɪ/   government—/ˈgʌvənmənt/

有些三音節的重音也落在第二音節上。例如：

adventure—/ədˈventʃə/   survival—/səˈvaɪvəl/
sufficient—/səˈfɪʃənt/   suspicion—/səsˈpɪʃən/

帶有-ion，-ian，-ous，-ence，-ient，-ure 等后綴的三音節詞，重音一般在第二個音節上。例如：

profession/prəˈfeʃən/   condition—/kənˈdɪʃən/
situation—/ˌsɪtjʊˈeɪʃən/   musician—/mjuːˈzɪʃən/
contagious—/kənˈteɪdʒəs/   experience—/ɪksˈpɪərɪəns/
sufficient—/səˈfɪʃənt/   adventure—/ədˈventʃə/

（三）多音節詞

這裡指四個或四個以上音節的詞。多音節詞的重音一般都在倒數第三個音節

上。例如：

democracy—/dɪˈmɒkrəsɪ/ anniversary—/ˌænɪˈvɜːsərɪ/
impossibility—/ɪmˌpɒsəˈbɪlɪtɪ/ psychology—/saɪˈkɒlədʒɪ/
international—/ˌɪntə(ː)ˈnæʃənəl/ photography—/fəˈtɒɡrəfɪ/

有些多音節的重音也落在倒數第二個音節上。

——以 -ic 結尾的單詞，如：economic—/ˌiːkəˈnɒmɪk/。

——以 -sion, -tion 結尾的單詞，如：revolution—/ˌrevəˈluːʃən/, discrimination—/dɪsˌkrɪmɪˈneɪʃən/。

（四）複合詞

複合詞是由兩個詞合成的。如在意義上仍保持兩個詞的獨立性，則兩詞都重讀，稱為並列重音。例如：White House（白宮），bus driver（公共汽車司機）。如兩詞在意義上聯繫緊密，產生一個新的意義時，第一個詞重讀，第二個詞則次重讀，稱為非並列重音。例如：handwriting 原意是「手寫」，hand 和 writing 合併，產生新義「書法」，hand 重讀，writing 次重讀。

1. 名詞性複合詞重音：

當複合詞由兩個名詞組成時，主重音一般放在第一個名詞上。在專有複合名詞中主重音一般放在第二個名詞上。例如：

basketball **pass**port **hand**bag **coffee** shop
New **York** United **States** Los **Angles** New **Zealand**

當複合詞由形容詞和名詞，或動詞和名詞組成時，主重音一般放在形容詞或動詞上。例如：

blackbird **black**board **short**cut **high**way
telltale **flash**light **turn**coat **lay**man

2. 形容詞性複合詞重音：

形容詞性複合詞的重音在第二個單詞上。例如：

old-**fashioned** bad-**tempered** sure-**footed** noble-**minded**

3. 動詞性複合詞重音：

此類複合詞的重音一般在動詞上。例如：

over**work** out**play** out**grow** under**stand**

註：黑體字部分為重讀單詞。

練習

朗讀下列單詞，標出單詞的音節及重音。

able table target telegram technology
fact favor effect effective inefficient

cure	curly	current	customer	curiosity
dear	danger	dangerous	declaration	deliberate
hair	habit	harmony	harmonious	historian
well-meant	warm-hearted	ill-mannered	website	weatherman
team spirit	outlive	out fight	outbreak	outdo
overburden	outline			

第 五 章　重音和節奏

漢語是一種聲調語言，而英語是一種以重讀為特點的語言。說漢語時，改變一個詞的聲調就改變了它的意思，如 ma 的四聲可分別為媽、麻、馬、罵四個不同意思的詞。因而，要學好漢語必須要掌握好四聲。而決定一個英語句子意思的因素除了元音、輔音的音質外，重音起了相當重要的作用。在一個句子中，重讀的詞就代表了句子的主要意思，如：I'm sorry I can't. ［很抱歉我不能（這樣做）。］這句中該重讀的詞是：sorry（抱歉）和 can't（不能），它們說出了句子的主要意思。此外，每個句子都有重讀和非重讀音節。此外，每個句子都有重讀、非重讀音節。這樣，輕輕重讀，高高低低形成起伏，也形成了英語動聽的節奏。

一、重音、節奏和語調的關係

在學習英語的過程中，無論是聽錄音還是看電影，你都會被英語美妙動聽的音調和節奏所吸引。就像音樂一樣，似乎英語也有著上下起伏、時快時慢的節奏和美麗的旋律。的確是這樣，英語給人的感覺像流水一樣，它像波浪一樣起伏，也像江河水一樣連續不斷。人們把流利的英語形容為「語流好」「節奏美」，就是這個道理。

在連貫說話時，語流的好壞、語調的正確與否主要決定於重音、節奏和語調。人們學習音樂的時候發現音樂有節拍，有自己的節奏和旋律。學說英語很像學音樂。英語的重音就是節拍，英語也有自己的節奏，英語的語調就是旋律。英語的單音和一個個音節像是音樂中的一個個音符。當然，只有讓這一個個音符跳動起來才能成為和諧的音樂，才能表達意思，抒發情感。同樣，只有讓這一個個音節跳動起來才能成為生動的語言，才能傳遞信息、交流感情。能使這些音節跳動起來成為完整語言的就是重音、節奏和語調。可以看出重音、節奏和語調這三者是一個有機的整體，是不可分割的。只是為了教學的便利，我們才分別來討論它們。

需要強調的另一點是，正確地發出每一個單音固然重要，但更重要的是語流。因為語流會直接影響交際時的效果。經常會遇到這樣的情況，某人單音發得很好，但用英語與英美人士交談時，效果卻不好。對方說聽不懂他的話，而他卻抱怨對方說話「又快又吞音節」。原因很簡單，是他自己沒有掌握好比單音更重要的重音、節奏和語調。

二、單詞重音

重音分單詞重音和語句重音兩種。關於單詞重音我們在第五課中已經概括地講過了。這裡再就單詞重音的規則作進一步說明。

只要是兩個音節以上的單詞都有一個重音，一些長的單詞有兩個重音，極少數的詞有三個重音。英語單詞重音的位置可以在任何一個音節上。在遇到一個新單詞時，一般情況下，最可靠的辦法是查字典，按照音標來讀音。不過，有一些單詞的重音是可以找到規律的，可以根據它們的拼法、前后綴等來判斷。

以下一些規則可供學習重音時參考：

（一）單詞重音規則

1. 在英語中，許多常用名詞和動詞重音往往在第一個音節上。例如：

'English   'language   'learner   'students
'lather   'mother   'teacher   'people
'sister   'brother   'family   'pretty

2. 帶有前綴 be-、in-、dis-、ex-、un-的雙音節和多音節詞，重音幾乎都落在第二或第三個音節上，因為英語的前綴是不重讀的。例如：

be'come   in'vite   dis'tract   ex'pect
dis'cover   in'form   ex'clude   un'do
be'gin   un'lock   dis'close   ex'plode

（注意：這些詞大多數是動詞。）

3. 英語所有詞的后綴都不重讀。

-ly   'comfortably 'carefully
-al   'national   inter'national
-tive   'active   pre'ventive
-ent/ant   'silent   'pleasant
-ic   he'roic   auto'matic

我們還可以看到，許多后綴可以決定重音的位置。在帶有后綴的長單詞（3~6個音節）中，重音總是在詞的中間，而不在第一或第二個音節上。

（1）以下這些后綴決定了重音的位置在后綴前的一個音節上：

-ive   im'pressive   -ic   photo'graphic
-ient   in'cipient   -ian   'median
-iant   'deviant   -ious   in'fectious
-ial   es'sential   -ity   oppor'tunity
-ion   in'vention

（2）單詞加上后綴-able 以后，重音保持不變：

re'ly   re'liable   de'test   de'testable

de'pend   de'pendable   'knowledge   'knowledgeable
a'dapt   a'daptable   'demonstrate   'demonstrable

（3）帶有以下這些后綴的單詞，重音落在倒數第四個音節上（前提是這些單詞必須有四個以上的音節）：

-ary   vo'cabulary   -acy   'intimacy
-ator   in'vestigator   -ory   'category
-mony   'ceremony

（4）英語中有一類詞拼寫是一樣的，但一個是名詞，一個是動詞。這類詞中，所有名詞的重音都在第一個音節上，所有動詞的重音都在第二個音節上。

例如：'contest（名詞）   con'test（動詞）

contest   contrast   discount   extract
import   conflict   digest   export
present   protest   record   produce
survey   refuse   subject   object

(二) 複合詞讀音規則

複合詞是指名詞+名詞，形容詞+名詞的組合。

以下是一些複合詞的讀音規則：

1. 名詞+名詞類。

複合詞的重音傾向於落在第一個音節上。例如：

a 'postman   a 'crossword   a 'newspaper   a 'blackbird
a 'windscreen   a 'grandmother   a 'teapot   a 'salesgirl
a 'keyboard   a 'chairman   a 'milkman   a 'doorkeeper

2. 形容詞+名詞類。

複合詞，如果兩個詞已變成一個合成詞，重音落在第一個音節上。如果兩個詞仍然是分開寫的，沒有變成一個詞，兩個詞都要重讀。請比較下列幾組句子：

This is the 'greenhouse.   This is the 'green 'house.
I see a 'hotdog.   I see a 'hot 'dog.
There is a 'blackbird in the garden. There is a 'black 'bird in the garden.

（注意：這三組句子中，每兩個句子的意思是不同的。）

三、語句重音

英語中每個單詞在單獨存在的時候都有重音（儘管單音節詞不打上重音符號），但單詞到了句子中就發生了變化。這個變化是，不一定每個單詞在句子中都有重音。那麼，哪些詞在句子中有重音？哪些詞在句子中沒有重音呢？

語句重音的規則是：一般來說，重要的詞重讀，不重要的詞不重讀。也可以這樣說，句子中實詞重讀，虛詞不重讀。

那麼，哪些是實詞，哪些是虛詞呢？

名詞、形容詞、數詞、動詞、副詞是實詞，一般要重讀。

冠詞、介詞、連詞、助動詞是虛詞，一般不重讀。

關於代詞需要單獨提一下，一般來說，多數代詞是不重讀的，如 her, me, it, them 等。但一部分代詞，如指示代詞 this 和疑問代詞 what，就要重讀。

懂得了這些規則對我們學習語流是有極大幫助的。你看，根據以上規則我們就可以對任何一個語句作語音分析了。以下這些句子中哪些詞重讀，哪些詞不重讀呢？例如：在 Janet has gone to school 這句中，Janet, gone, school 三個詞是實詞，要重讀。而 has, to 兩個詞是虛詞，要弱讀。

以下句子重讀的情況是這樣的：

'Janet has 'gone to school.

I 'saw your 'brother yesterday.

'Can I 'carry your suitcase?

'Would you 'like a 'glass of beer?

'Have you 'heard about John?

I must be going. My 'wife is 'waiting for me at the 'corner of the street.

顯然，分析重讀和弱讀是非常必要的，因為這是我們朗讀所有句子的依據。另外，從以上例句可以看出，重讀音節出現的間隔是很有規律的。每隔一段就出現一個重音。兩個重音之間隔著不同數目的非重讀音節，構成了英語上下起伏、有規律的節奏。這些節奏不但很均衡，而且有節拍。這就是為什麼可以打著拍子學習英語語調的道理。例如：

Janet has gone to school.

此句中有三個重讀音節：Janet, gone 和 school。每個重音有一拍，每拍之間間隔是一樣的。而在兩拍之間必須把非重讀音節讀完。這就是英語的節奏。對於中國的英語學習者來說，最困難的不是重讀音節，而是非重讀音節。我們很容易把重讀音節和非重讀音節讀得一樣重，這樣就破壞了節奏，聽起來就不像英語了。Janet has gone to school，是個比較容易的句子，因為每兩個重讀音節之間只有一個非重讀音節。但例句中的最後一句 My wife is waiting for me at the corner of the street，就不一樣了。句子重讀音節只有四個：wife, wait（ing）, corner 和 street。但兩個重讀音節之間卻隔著好幾個非重讀音節，如 waiting for me at the corner 中，wait 和 corner 之間就隔著五個非重讀音節。也就是說，這個句子可以打四拍，每拍之間間隔是一樣的。而在兩拍之間必須把所有非重讀音節讀完。這時候就要求我們讀得輕而快，還要求我們用弱讀形式，否則就不可能讀完。如果讀慢了、讀重了，就必然會破壞節奏。

因此我們需要培養一種能力，這種能力使我們可以把句子說得又清楚，又自然，又有節奏。如何來培養這種能力呢？語音學家們設計了許多既簡單又有成效

的方法。我們可以採用一些最適合中國人的方法來進行練習。

方法一：

練習重讀，先從短的詞組讀起，逐漸擴展到長的詞組。

a book

a good book

a very good book

a very good textbook

a very good school textbook

This is a very good school textbook.

a cup

an empty cup

an empty cup and saucer

an empty cup and a broken saucer.

two empty cups and a broken saucer

There are two empty cups and a broken saucer.

方法二：

日常生活中的語言是五彩繽紛、千姿百態的，很不容易找到規律。語音學家們經過努力，收集大量可貴的資料，在人們最常用的語言中，總結歸納出了一系列重音節奏模式（簡稱重音模式）。這些重音模式是我們學習重音、體會節奏、掌握語調的絕妙教材。例如：

'Sit down!

'Sing a song.

以上兩個英語句子雖然都很短，仔細分析后，可以看出它們屬於兩種不同類型。第一個句子中兩個詞都要重讀。第二個句子中兩個重讀的詞中間有一個非重讀的詞。因此語音學家們就把它們歸為不同的重音模式。為了更形象地表達出來，他們用大方塊表示重讀音節，用小方塊表示非重讀音節。例如：

'Sit down!

□　　□

'Sing a song.

□　　□　□

也有些語音學家用大圓圈表示重讀音節，用小圓圈表示非重讀音節。例如：

'Sit down!

　O　　O

'Sing a song.

　O　o　O

除了用形象的符號來表示不同的重音模式外，語音學家們還借用音樂的方法來表示。這樣我們不但可以看到不同的重音模式，還可以像唱歌一樣哼出不同的節奏來。一種方法是用大 DA 表示重讀音節，用小 da 表示非重讀音節。例如：

'Sit down!

DA DA

'Sing a song.

　DA da DA

也有些語音學家用大 MM 表示重讀音節，用小 mm 表示非重讀音節。例如：

'Sit down!

MM MM

'Sing a song.

MM mm MM

還有一些語音書中用了其他的符號，這裡就不贅述了。

四、重音模式

我們採用大小方塊的形式分別表示重讀和非重讀音節。同時採用 DA 和 da 的符號分別表示重讀和非重讀音節以便吟誦。

應該怎樣來練習重音模式呢？我們先以模式 A 和模式 B 為例說明。

例如：

1. 重音模式 A □■□□□

示例：（1）I've 'eaten them all.

　　　（2）We 'had to do it.

重音模式 A 告訴我們：

句子中有五個音節，其中第二個音節是重讀音節，需要重讀，其他四個音節都是非重讀音節，不需要重讀。它的重音模式是：弱—強—弱—弱—弱。示例 I've eaten them all. 和 We had to do it. 完全符合重音模式 A。因此，我們可以把重音模式 A □■□□□用到這兩個例句中去。應該這樣讀這兩個句子：

I've 'eaten them all.

□　■□　□　□

We 'had to do it.

□　■　□□　□

或者

I've 'eaten them all.

da　DAda　da　　da

We 'had to do it.
da DA da da da

2. 重音模式 B □ □ □ □ □ □

示例：（1）She 'wanted to write to him.

（2）It's 'not what I asked you for.

重音模式 B 告訴我們：

句子中有七個音節，其中第二和第五兩個音節是重讀音節，需要重讀，其他五個音節都是非重讀音節，不需要重讀。它的重音模式是：弱—強—弱—弱—強—弱—弱。示例 She wanted to write to him. 和 It's not what I asked you for. 完全符合重音模式 B。因此，我們可以把重音模式 B □ □ □ □ □ □ □用到這兩個例句中去。

6. 應該這樣讀這兩個句子：

She 'wanted to write to him.
□ □ □ □ □ □ □

It's 'not what I asked you for.
□ □ □ □ □ □ □

或者

She 'wanted to write to him.
da DAda daDA da da

It's 'not what I asked you for.
da DA da da DA da da

常見的重音模式有：

模式 1 □ □

示範：'Speak up.
　　　　□ □
　　　　DA DA

模式 2 □ □ □

示範：'Do it flow.
　　　□ □ □
　　　DA da DA

模式 3 □ □ □

示範：I think so.
　　　□ □ □
　　　da DA da

第五章　重音和節奏

111

模式 4 □ □ □ □

示範：I've heard of it.
　　　　□　□　□□
　　　　da　DA　da da

模式 5 □ □ □ □

示範：Send him a card.
　　　□　　□　　□□
　　　DA　da　da DA

模式 6 □ □ □ □ □

示範：I gave it to her.
　　　□ □ □ □ □
　　　da DA da da da

模式 7 □ □ □ □

示範：I want to know.
　　　□ □ □ □
　　　da DA da DA

模式 8 □ □ □ □ □

示範：I'll finish it flow.
　　　□ □□ □ □
　　　da DAda da DA

模式 9 □ □ □ □ □

示範：Carry it away.
　　　□□ □ □□
　　　DAda da daDA

模式 10 □ □ □ □ □

示範：I 'wanted you to know.
　　　□ □□　□ □ □
　　　da DAda　da da DA

模式 11 □ □ □ □

示範：It 'doesn't matter.
　　　□ □□　□□
　　　da DAda DAda

模式 12 □ □ □ □ □ □

示範：I'll 'borrow another one.
　　　□　□□　□□　□
　　　da　DAda　daDAda　da

模式 13 □ □ □ □ □ □ □

示範：I 'think he did it beautifully.
　　　　　□ □　□ □ □ □□□□
　　　　　da DA da da da DAdadada

模式 14 □ □ □ □ □

示範：Finish it if you can.
　　　　□□ □□ □
　　　　DAda dada da DA

模式 15 □ □ □ □ □

示範：It's 'not the 'one I want.
　　　　　□ □　□ □ □ □
　　　　　da DA da　DA da DA

模式 16 □ □ □ □ □ □

示範：It isn't the 'same as before.
　　　　□ □□ □ □ □ □□
　　　　da DAda da DA da daDA

模式 17 □ □ □ □ □ □ □ □

示範：I 'don't suppose you'll 'overlook my point.
　　　　□□　□　□□　□□□ □ □
　　　　da DA　da　dada　DAdada da DA

模式 18 □ □ □ □ □ □

示範：She 'married 'Mary's brother.
　　　　□ □□　□□　□□
　　　　da DAda　DAda　DAda

模式 19 □ □ □ □ □ □ □ □

示範：I 'think that he 'wants us to take him there.
　　　　□□　□　□　□ □□ □ □
　　　　da DA　da da　DA da da DA da da

模式 20 □ □ □ □ □ □

示範：'When are you going away?
　　　　□　□　□　□□ □□
　　　　DA　da　da　dada daDA

模式 21 □ □ □ □ □ □

示範：She 'looks a 'little 'pale to me.
　　　　□　□　□□□　□　□
　　　　da　DA　da DAda DA da DA

模式 22 □□□□□□□□□

示範：He 'says that he 'wants us to 'take it away.
　　　　□□　　□□　　□　　□□　　□□□
　　　　da DA　da da　DA　da da　DA da daDA

練習

1. 用課文中提到的方法一練習以下短語和句子。

示範：

a cloth

a piece of cloth

a piece of white cloth

a large piece of white cloth

a large piece of pure white cloth

This is a large piece of pure white cloth.

（1）a cloth/a piece of cloth/a piece of white cloth/a large piece of white cloth/a large piece of pure white cloth/This is a large piece of pure white cloth.

（2）a boy/a naughty boy/a very naughty boy/a very naughty English schoolboy/Jack is a very naughty English schoolboy.

（3）a telephone/a public telephone/two public telephones/two public telephones on Platform 4/two new public telephones on Platform 4/There are two new public telephones on Platform 4.

（4）a clock/my friend's clock/the hands of my friend's clock/the metal hands of my friend's clock/the two broken metal hands of my friend's clock.

（5）a desk/an oak desk/an oak desk with drawers/a polished oak desk with drawers/a polished oak desk with large drawers.

2. 朗讀含有以下后綴的單詞，然后找出它們的規律。

后綴-ness

kindness	laziness	politeness	shyness
happiness	sadness	rudeness	ugliness
meanness	weakness	friendliness	sweetness
illness	tiredness	selfishness	cleverness

后綴-less

breathless	useless	careless	tactless
colourless	fearless	endless	fatherless
powerless	penniless	homeless	faultless

| meaningless | motherless | shapeless | thoughtless |

后缀 -tion
organization	pronunciation	dictation	description
explanation	punctuation	modernization	instruction
direction	socialization	nationalization	intention

后缀 -ture
adventure	literature	agriculture	mixture
architecture	culture	nature	picture
feature	structure	signature	lecture
departure	furniture	future	temperature

3. 朗讀下列各組單詞，注意重音的變化。

'politics	po'litical	poli'tician
'democrat	de'mocracy	demo'cratic
'personal	per'sonify	perso'nality
'hypocrite	hy'pocrisy	hypo'critical
'photograph	pho'tographer	photo'graphical
'benefit	be'neficent	bene'ficial
'mechanism	me'chanical	mecha'nician
'intellect	in'telligence	intel'lectual
'family	fa'miliar	famili'arity
'telegraph	te'legraphy	tele'graphic
'particle	par'ticular	particu'larity
'competence	com'petitor	compe'tition
'diplomat	di'plomacy	diplo'matic

4. 朗讀以下句子，注意 I, me, we, us, you, he, him, she, it, they, them 等人稱代詞通常不重讀。

(1) give it to her　　　send him away　　　take her out
　　write them a letter　　put it down　　　bring her round
　　wake me up　　　　pick me up　　　　give it up
　　tell her the story

(2) Tell him where we are going.
　　Ask her if she wants to go with us.
　　He brought me some flowers.
　　He enjoyed himself in Tibet.
　　We blamed ourselves for doing it.

Will you show me the way?

Phone me if you need me.

It told them the truth.

Tell Mother I won't be back for dinner.

She bought him some chocolates.

5. 朗讀與欣賞。

(1)

> Make new friends, but keep the old;
> Those are silver, these are gold.
> New-made friendships, like new wine,
> Age will mellow and refine.
> Friendships that have stood the test—
> Time and change—are surely best;
> Brow may wrinkle, hair grow gray,
> Friendship never knows decay.
> For mid old friends, tried and true,
> Once more we our youth renew.
> But old friends, alas! may die,
> New friends must their places supply.
> Cherish friendship in your breast—
> New is good, but old is best;
> Make new friends, but keep the old;
> Those are silver, these are gold.

(2)

> A Happy Marriage
>
> A man was telling one of his friends the secret of his contented married life. 「My wife makes all the small decisions,」 he explained, 「and I make all the big ones, so we never interfere in each other's business and never get annoyed withe each other. We have no complaints and no arguments.」
>
> 「That sounds reasonable,」 answered his friend sympathetically. 「All what sort of decisions does your wife make?」
>
> 「Well,」 answered the man, 「she decides what jobs I apply for, what sort of house we live in, what furniture we have, where we go for our holidays, and things like that.」
>
> His friend was surprised. 「Oh?」 he said, 「And what do you consider important decision then?」
>
> 「Well,」 answered the man, 「I decide who should be Prime Minister, whether we should increase our help to poor countries, what we should do about the atom bomb, and things like that.」

第六章 弱讀

　　一般來說，英語句子中需要弱讀的是一些虛詞，即沒有完整的詞彙意義但有語法意義或功能意義的詞。通俗地說，就是那些沒有多少實在意義、在句子中不能獨立擔當句子成分的詞，如冠詞、一部分代詞（人稱代詞）、單音節介詞和單音節連詞。而句子中的實詞通常要重讀，也就是名詞、實義動詞、形容詞、副詞、一部分代詞（指示代詞、反身代詞、疑問代詞）和感嘆詞。

　　下面我們就按照詞的分類，結合實例來看一看英語中常見的需要弱讀的單詞都有哪些。

一、冠詞的弱讀

1. a /ə/, an /ən/

a ruler, an apple, an honest man

a European company

What a shame!

An apple a day keeps the doctor away.

2. the /ðə/, /ðɪ/

What's the name of this movie?

I saw him crossing the bridge the other day.

二、介詞的弱讀

1. at /ət/

I'm looking at the picture.

Jack's still at work.

I'll meet you at the gate of the school.

You'll see a restaurant at the corner.

2. for /fə/

Is this book for me?

Our friendship will last for ever!

Getting up early will be good for you.

3. from /frəm/

I can't tell Lily from Lucy.

I've just received an invitation card from Tom.

He's a visitor from South Korea.

4. of　/əv/

One of the keys is missing.

This moon cake is made of flour, cheese, sugar and eggs.

I've ever heard of it many times.

5. to　/tə/

This road leads to Paris.

He was wet to the skin.

Things are going from bad to worse.

6. than　/ðən/

He is twice heavier than his wife.

My aunt stayed here for more than a week.

三、連詞的弱讀

1. and　/ənd, ən/

Five and six is eleven.

It is raining cats and dogs.

Give Mary six and a penny.

2. as　/əz/

as far as I know

It seems as if his answer is correct.

Do as what the teacher has told you.

I must leave now, as it's already eight o'clock.

3. but　/bət/

It's not good-looking but useful and handy.

It's raining heavily outside, but I'll go out as well.

Jim's clever but not very careful.

4. or　/ə/

He will be away for one or two weeks.

What would you prefer, tea or coffee?

5. than　/ðən/

It's much more difficult than I thought.

The cost of the repairs was cheaper than I thought.

四、連接詞 that 的弱讀

1. that 引導主語從句

It's possible that we can accomplish this project at last.

It's a pity that you didn't join us in the picnic.

2. that 引導表語從句

The reason is that he has not got enough money.

It appears that he has some heavy news in his heart.

3. that 引導賓語從句

I told him that he was too careless.

He said that he was not intended to hurt you.

4. that 引導同位語從句

The fact that Great Britain is made up of three countries is still unknown to many people.

The suggestion that students should listen and practice more is worth considering.

五、代詞的弱讀

（一）人稱代詞的弱讀

1. he /hɪ, ɪ/

He told me a secret about the boss.

He is one of the best doctors in the city.

2. she /ʃɪ/

What did she say?

She said She was not in at that time.

She doesn't like bananas, does she?

3. his /ɪz/

I like his beautiful handwriting.

Is this his umbrella?

4. her /hə, ə/

I gave her a box of chocolate for her birthday last year.

She's got her ticket to her hometown.

Her answer shocked her teacher.

5. me /mɪ/

Could you please pass me the ball?

Show me a picture of your family.

Tell me what your favorite color is.

6. him /ɪm/

Send him my best regards.

Tell him to come on time.

I don't know him and I don't want to know him.

7. them /ðəm/

We saw them in the supermarket yesterday.

Give them all these old clothes.

If I see them, I'll tell them the truth.

8. us /æ, s/

They told us to go.

I wonder if they saw us on the street this morning.

The local hosts gave us a warm welcome.

(二) 關係代詞的弱讀

1. that /ðət/

All that is needed is a supply of oil.

The thief handed everything that he had stolen to the police.

Did you see the letter that came yesterday?

2. who /hʊ/

Do you know the boy who lives here?

I don't know who the old man is.

I saw the boy who lost his schoolbag.

六、動詞的弱讀

(一) 助動詞的弱讀

1. do /də, d/

What do you want to do?

Where do you usually buy fruits?

Do you really agree with him?

Why do you work so hard?

2. does /dəz/

What does she do for a living?

Where does this road lead to?

Where does Diana live?

3. has /həz, z/; have /həv/; had /həd, d/

Has the milkman come?

We have finished our homework ahead of time.

When Tom had finished, he left without saying a single word.

(二) 情態動詞的弱讀

1. can /kən/

What can I do for you, Madam?

I can see it quite clearly.

Can you do me a favor?

2. could /kəd/

I could touch my toes.

What could we do to address the financial crisis?

How I wish that I could fly!

3. shall /ʃəl/

Where shall we meet?

Shall I see you tomorrow or the day after tomorrow?

I shall be fifteen next month.

4. should /ʃəd/

I wonder what I should do.

You should be more careful next time, good boy.

Everyone should try to do more to help others.

5. would /wəd, d/

What would you like?

What would we do?

6. must /məst/

He must leave for the airport now.

You must eat it at once as it is still fresh.

That work must be done at once.

(三) 系動詞的弱讀

1. be /bɪ/

Don't be late again.

Do be quiet when others are speaking.

I'll be there soon.

2. am /əm/

What am I to do?

Where am I now?

3. are /ə/

Are you still there?

My parents are out.

What are you doing?

Are you ready to start now?

4. been   /bɪn/

Jim has been in Beijing for a long time.

All the work's been done.

I've been cheated.

5. was   /wəz/

What was she talking about?

Was anyone hurt?

He said his father was an engineer.

七、其他一些單詞的弱讀

1. to   /tʊ, tə/

The girl came to after a while.（adv.）

I'd like to go with you.（adv.）

2. there   /ðə/

There comes the bus.（adv.）

There is a dog under the tree.（adv.）

They have moved somewhere near there.（n.）

3. not   /nt/

It doesn't matter.

I haven't finished my homework yet.

4. some   /səm, sm/

I've got some presents for you.（adj.）

Some twenty passengers were killed in the road accident.（adv.）

His mastery of the language has improved some.（adv.）

練習

1. 朗讀下列句子，注意句子中需要弱讀的單詞。

Shall we go to the cinema?

Is there a post office near here?

I have nothing but a warm heart.

Where had it disappeared to?

Your mother is such a good cook.

I asked him for some salt in vain.

Would you like some coffee or tea?

I am willing to go to the zoo with you.

We stopped there for a swim.

Where were you when I called you?

You always give us advice on what to do.

I shall go and see you tomorrow morning.

It looks as if you know the truth very well.

You should be more careful next time.

Time is a bird for ever on the wing.

2. 你知道下列英語中的諺語所對應的漢語意思嗎？仔細朗讀並注意句中需要弱讀的單詞。

Do in Rome as the Romans do.（入鄉隨俗。）

Do not wash dirty linen in public.（家醜不可外揚。）

In for a penny, in for a pound.（一不做，二不休。）

Never offer to teach fish to swim.（切莫班門弄斧。）

Failure is the mother of success.（失敗是成功之母。）

It is better to do well than to say well.（說得好不如做得好。）

A straight foot is not afraid of a crooked shoe.（身正不怕影子斜。）

Count not your chickens before they are hatched.（不要過早樂觀。）

A bird is known by its note and a man by his talk.（聞其歌知其鳥，聽其言知其人。）

A man knows his companion in a long journey and a little inn.（路遙知馬力，日久見人心。）

3. 朗讀下面兩則小故事，注意故事中需要弱讀的部分。

The King and His Stories

Once upon a time there was a king. He liked to write short stories, but his stories were not good. As people were afraid of him, they all said that his stories were good.

One day the king showed his stories to a very famous novel writer. He waited for the writer and wished that he could praise these stories. But the writer said that his stories were so bad that he should throw them into fire. The king got very angry with him and soon sent him to prison.

After some time, the king decided to set the writer free. Again he showed him some of his new stories and asked what he thought of them.

After reading them, the writer at once turned to the soldiers and said,「Take me back to prison, please.」

The English Teacher

  The cave had started out simply as a crack in the cliff, a possibility of a shelter from the wind and rain. It ran deeper than expected, and the battered and drenched man crept along, feeling his way. He had obviously been running, and not just from the rain, as he struggled in vain to quiet his breathing which came in ragged gasps. Every couple of feet a gasp for breath would be a gasp of pain, as he scraped his already ragged knee on the side of the cave. After twenty feet, the opening was dim light behind him. Blood trickled unnoticed from a gash that ran up his right leg from his knee, and then soaked into what remained of his pants where it caked on with what was already there. No longer visible was his haggard face, drawn and pale from pain and exhaustion, pinched in with visible determination. Hair made his face rough, and blended into his close cut hair, which was missing along with part of his scalp above his left ear, while his left eye was nearly swollen shut. What remained from his shirt and pants were in shreds, and he bled from a dozen minor cuts, not as bad as that on his knee but, still sure to cause considerable pain. Some of the cuts were dirty, obviously from falls taken while running over rocks, but others were smooth and equally obviously not the result of any accident.

第七章　輔音連綴

第一節　輔音連綴

一、輔音連綴

在同一意群內，如果有兩個或兩個以上的輔音音素結合在一起，這種語音現象稱為輔音連綴。輔音連綴可發生在詞首、詞中和詞尾。在元音前，連綴的輔音不超過三個；在元音后，連綴的輔音不超過四個。讀輔音連綴時，前面的輔音必須讀得輕一些、短促些，各個輔音之間不能夾入元音/ə/。音與音之間要銜接緊密、快速，過渡自然。

例如：stopped—/stɒpt/一詞中的/st/和/pt/，six—/sɪks/一詞中的/ks/。

二、詞首輔音連綴發音要領

詞首輔音連綴發音時需要注意：第一個輔音剛一發出，立即作好發第二個音的準備。發音時第一個輔音的發音要輕而短，第二個輔音的發音要重而長，注意力要在第二個輔音的發音上。兩個音連接緊密，不要在兩個輔音之間添加元音，也不能吞沒輔音連綴中的任何一個輔音。

試朗讀下面的例詞：

/sm/：	smart	smear	smile	smoke
/sn/：	snail	snake	snap	snow
/sl/：	slight	slave	slang	slim
/sw/：	sweet	swim	sweat	swift
/sk/：	sky	skin	skite	
/spr/：	spring	sprite	spray	
/bl/：	black	blue	blind	
/br/：	bread	brave	bright	
/pl/：	play	plot	plant	
/pr/：	pray	print	press	
/dr/：	drop	draw	drive	
/tr/：	tray	tree	travel	
/tw/：	twin	twelve	twinkle	
/gl/：	glass	glance	gloom	

/gr/：grass　　　great　　　grape
/kl/：clap　　　click　　　clock
/kr/：cross　　　cream　　　crime
/kw/：quick　　　quite　　　quiet
/fl/：fly　　　flag　　　flash
/fr/：free　　　from　　　friend
/θr/：throw　　　three　　　thread
/ʃr/：shrug　　　shrink　　　shrimp

三、詞尾輔音連綴發音要領

詞尾輔音連綴發音時和詞首輔音連綴相同時需要注意的問題，即：不要在兩個輔音之間添加元音，不可吞沒任何一個輔音。

試朗讀下面的例詞：

/ft/：lift　　　left　　　theft
/st/：nest　　　list　　　first
/ld/：mild　　　field　　　guild
/nd/：second　　　find　　　lend
/nz/：bronze　　　Benz　　　lens
/ks/：fix　　　mix　　　tax
/kst/：next　　　fixed　　　mixed

然而，更多的詞尾輔音連綴卻是出現在動詞或名詞詞尾加-ed/-d 或 -es/-s 時。以下就是相應輔音連綴的發音規則。

（一）加-es/s

動詞或名詞詞尾加-es/-s 的輔音連綴需遵守「清清濁濁」的讀音規則：

1. 以清輔音結尾（除/s/、/t/、/ʃ/、/tʃ/外）的名詞加復數詞尾及動詞加第三人稱單數-es/-s 時，應發成清輔音/s/。例如：

名詞—desks, maps, roofs, months, ducks, chicks, drops, lamps。
動詞—likes, makes, stops, takes, breaks, seeks, thinks, keeps。

2. 以濁輔音（除/d/、/z/、/dʒ/外）或元音結尾的名詞加復數詞尾及動詞加第三人稱單數-es/-s 時，應發成濁輔音/z/。例如：

名詞—labs, cells, names, knives, pens, eggs, measures, movies。
動詞—robs, loves, claims, drives, digs, opens, cheers, circles。

3. 以/s/、/ʃ/、/tʃ/、/z/、/dʒ/結尾的名詞加復數詞尾及動詞加第三人稱單數-es/-s 時，應發成/ɪz/。例如：

名詞—faces, noses, roses, classes, matches, brushes, bridges, oranges。

4. 以清輔音/t/或濁輔音/d/結尾的名詞后加復數或動詞后加第三人稱單數形式-s時分別讀成/ts/或/dz/。例如：

名詞—sheets, shirts, boots, habits, deeds, birds, lands, grades。
動詞—meets, lifts, costs, writes, speeds, leads, reads, aids。

(二) 加-ed

動詞或名詞詞尾加-ed的輔音連綴也需遵守「清清濁濁」的讀音規則：

1. 以清輔音結尾（/t/除外）的動詞，詞尾加-ed發清輔音/t/。例如：cooked, jumped, guessed, clashed, laughed, watched, washed。

2. 以濁輔音（/d/除外）或元音結尾的動詞，詞尾加-ed發濁輔音/d/。例如：robbed, lived, spoiled, seemed, played。

3. 以/t/、/d/結尾的動詞詞尾加-ed讀作/ɪd/。例如：fitted, created, wanted, waited, handed, founded, minded, surrounded。

四、音的濁化

/s/后面的爆破清輔音/p/、/t/、/k/讀成濁輔音/b/、/d/、/g/，這種現象就叫做音的濁化。發生音的濁化需要同時滿足以下條件：① /sp/、/st/、/sk/出現在某一元音前面；② /sp/、/st/、/sk/和該元音在同一個音節中。濁化現象的發音要領是：第一個摩擦音/s/發音極其短促，發音后立即閉緊雙唇發/p/，或立即抬起舌尖抵住齒齦發/t/音，或抬起舌根貼住軟腭發/k/音，切忌添加元音，并同后面的元音一起拼讀成各個單詞；連綴中的第二個清輔音雖是爆破音但發音時不送氣，而且聲帶要振動，產生濁化，即讀成/b/、/d/、/g/。例如：

/sp/: spite   spirit   speed   speak   spring
/st/: start   study   sting   stock   understand
/sk/: sky   skirt   skate   school   scholarship

注意：詞尾處的/-s-/+清輔音連綴不必濁化，因為它們出現在元音后面。例如：next, ask, fast, last, dust。

練習

1. 讀下面的單詞，注意詞首的輔音連綴及音的濁化。

black	brand	please	present	dragon	translate
grave	glad	clear	crack	question	quake
flee	free	twenty	trick	thrive	shrink
smog	smile	snore	slip	slender	swear
spare	special	street	strike	skill	scheme

2. 朗讀下面的單詞，注意詞尾的輔音連綴。

名詞	ships	lips	chips	truths	proofs
	clubs	legs	bags	rooms	cousins
	lids	beds	bottles	chairs	pencils
	lads	plums	glasses	dishes	advantages
動詞	urges	lets	sits	lasts	assists
	saves	goes	does	flies	lies
	closes	advises	finishes	changes	blesses
	wastes	departs	corrects	competes	affords
	passed	booked	chopped	finished	reached
	lighted	granted	feared	believed	demanded

第二節　失去爆破和部分失去爆破

一、爆破音

爆破音是指發音器官在口腔中形成阻礙，然后氣流衝破阻礙而發出的音。這類音共有6個，即/p/，/b/，/t/，/d/，/k/和/g/。

二、失去爆破和部分失去爆破

當兩個爆破音相鄰，發前一爆破音時，氣流不必衝破阻礙，而只是發音器官在口腔中形成阻礙，並稍做停頓。也就是說，做好要發出這個爆破音的準備，但不要發出音來，這樣的發音過程叫做「失去爆破」。

當一個爆破音與隨后的其他輔音相鄰，發此爆破音時，發音器官並不形成阻礙而只形成一個很狹小的縫隙，讓氣流從縫隙中流出，這種爆破是不完全的，這樣的發音過程叫做「部分失去爆破」。

三、失去爆破和部分失去爆破的讀音規則

（劃線部分讀音失去爆破或部分失去爆破）

（一）爆破音+爆破音的發音要領：

當六個爆破音中的任何兩個音相遇或相連接時，前一爆破音失去爆破。例如：

單詞中：	blackboard	lamppost	goodbye
	football	September	postcard
短語中：	a good time	a red tie	sit down
	next book	keep quiet	pocket book

句子中：Glad to meet you.
He has a bad cold today.
This is a good picture.

(二) 爆破音+摩擦音/破擦音的發音要領：

爆破音后面如出現摩擦音/f, v/、/θ, ð/、/s, z/、/ʃ, ʒ/、/r, h/和破擦音/tʃ, dʒ/時，此爆破音部分失去爆破，只能聽到極輕微的爆破聲，主要聽到的是后面的摩擦音或破擦音。例如：

單詞中： midst   absent   object   picture
potful   advice   obvious   thanks

短語中： a big change   a big horse
a good child   a red shirt
a black jacket   old friend

句子中： You may keep the change.
The third chair is broken.
Have you read the book about that child?

(三) 爆破音+鼻音的發音分兩種情況：

第一種情況：爆破音/t/或/d/后面緊跟著鼻輔音/n/或/m/，且兩個輔音能組合成一個音節時，爆破須由在口腔中實施改為在鼻腔中實施。這種輔音組合在語音學裡叫做鼻腔爆破。如：cotton/ˈkɒtn/中的/tn/，person/ˈpɜːsn/中的/sn/就得採取上述方法發音。這是因為發爆破音/t/或/d/時因受后面鼻輔音/n/或/m/的影響爆破部位有所改變，/t/或/d/的爆破改道從鼻子裡出來了。發音時鼻子裡（而不是口腔）會有一種充氣及發麻的感覺。

常見錯誤：發這樣的組合時往往在兩個輔音/tn/或/dn/之間錯誤地加入一個元音/ə/，讀成/tən/或/dən/。

糾正辦法：使/tn/或/dn/在同一部位（即齒齦）同時發音。關鍵是舌尖要緊緊貼住齒齦不動（不能放下來），然后使勁用氣流衝擊軟腭使之下降而打開鼻腔通道，爆破聲就會自然地和鼻輔音/n/一起從鼻子裡出來了。試讀下列單詞：

fasten   beaten   written   frighten   forgotten
pardon   hidden   broaden   garden   widen

第二種情況：爆破音/t/、/d/在鼻音/m/、/n/的前面，且不屬於同一個音節時，部分失去爆破，只能聽到極輕微的爆破聲，主要聽到的是后面的鼻音。例如：

單詞中： postman   partner   dustman   fortnight
admit   flatmate   admire   goodness

短語中： fat man   round moon

red meat　　　　　a just man
good memory　　　important meeting

句子中：Good morning, sir.
　　　　Good night and have a sweet dream.
　　　　No news is good news.
　　　　It doesn't matter.
　　　　Sorry, I don't know.

（四）爆破音+舌側音的發音分兩種情況：

第一種情況：爆破音/t/或/d/后面緊跟著舌側音/l/，且可以組合為一個音節。爆破音/t/、/d/和舌邊音/l/的發音部位相同，都在上齒齦這一部位。不同的是發爆破音/t/、/d/時除舌尖貼住齒齦外，舌的兩側也要貼住上顎的兩側；發舌側音/l/時則相反，舌的兩側要離開上顎，以便聲音從舌的一側或兩側泄出。由於發音部位相同，/t/、/l/或/d/、/l/在一起時兩音應同時發音，舌尖頂住齒齦不動，只要在發/l/時使舌的兩側下垂，使/t/、/d/的爆破通過/l/泄出。這種發音方法在語音學中就叫做「舌側爆破」。當爆破音/t/、/d/從舌側泄出時，可以感到腮部的兩邊因強烈送氣而鼓起。發此音最重要的是要和/təu/、/dəu/區別開來。例如：

little　　　battle　　　settle　　　cattle　　　bottle
riddle　　　bundle　　　handle　　　model　　　needle

第二種情況：爆破音/t/、/d/在舌側音/l/的前面，且不屬於同一音節時，部分失去爆破，只能聽到極輕微的爆破聲，主要聽到的是后面的舌側音。例如：

單詞中：outline　　　firstly　　　lastly　　　mostly
　　　　outlook　　　loudly　　　friendly　　　rapidly
短語中：red lips　　　　　at lunch
　　　　at least　　　　　at leisure
the first lesson at last
句子中：Can you speak it loudly?
　　　　You can come to my house at lunch time.
　　　　He's going away for at least a week.
　　　　I don't like it.

練習

1. 朗讀下列單詞，注意黑體字部分的讀音。

text　　　　output　　　practice　　dictate　　　outcome
cupboard　　distinct　　bacteria　　notebook　　background
mindless　　optical　　　outside　　　fraction　　badminton

cat –nap   costly   restless   itself   bookshelf

2. 朗讀下列短語，注意黑體字部分的讀音。

cut down   first room
help them   write down
keep quiet   blind date
make sure   loud cheers
good chance   second hand

3. 朗讀下列句子，注意黑體字部分的讀音。

（1）Keep quiet, please.

（2）Someone is waiting for you at the front door.

（3）「Take care of yourself」, said my mother.

（4）We are good friends.

（5）Would you like to drink some water?

（6）A big shower came and Alice ran into a street shop.

（7）Zero is neither an even number nor an odd number.

（8）Let's review the first lesson.

（9）Have a good sleep!

4. 讀下列繞口令，注意其中的不完全爆破現象。

（1）Few free fruit flies fly from flames.

（2）The great Greek grape growers grow great Greek grapes.

（3）Too many teenagers tend to waste their time watching television.

（4）I like to ride my light white bike, and fly a white light kite with my wife.

（5）A big black bug bit a big black bear and made the big black bear bleed blood.

（6）There is no need to light a night light on a light night like tonight, for a bright night light is just like a slight light.

（7）A pleasant peasant keeps a pleasant pheasant and both the peasant and the pheasant are having a pleasant time together.

（8）Bill was beating a big beast with his big fist, and his big fist was badly bitten by the big beast.

5. 讀下列兩則故事，特別要注意其中不完全爆破音的發音方式。

Alibaba and the Forty Thieves

Three men were discussing at a bar about coincidences. The first man said,「My wife was reading *A Tale of Two Cities* and she gave birth to twins.」

「That's funny,」the second man remarked,「My wife was reading *The Three Musketeers* and she gave birth to triplets.」

On hearing that, the third man shouted,「God, I have to rush home!」

When asked what the problem was, he exclaimed,「When I left the house, my wife was reading *Alibaba and the Forty Thieves*!!!」

The Unicorn in the Garden
by *James Thurber*

Once upon a sunny morning, a man who sat in a breakfast nook looked up from his scram bled eggs to see a white unicorn with a golden horn quietly cropping the roses in the garden. The man went up to the bedroom where his wife was still asleep and woke her.「There's a unicorn in the garden,」he said,「eating roses.」She opened one unfriendly eye and looked at him.「The unicorn is a mythical beast,」she said, and turned her back on him. The man walked slowly downstairs and out into the garden. The unicorn was still there; he was now browsing among the tulips.「Here, unicorn,」said the man and pulled up a lily and gave it to him. The unicorn ate it gravely. With a high heart, because there was a unicorn in his garden, the man went upstairs and roused his wife again.「The unicorn,」he said,「ate a lily.」His wife sat up in bed and looked at him, coldly.「You are a booby,」she said,「and I am going to have you put in a booby-hatch.」The man, who never liked the words「booby」and「booby-hatch」, and who liked them even less on a shining morning when there was a unicorn in the garden, thought for a moment.「We'll see about that,」he said. He walked over to the door. 「He has a golden horn in the middle of his forehead,」he told her. Then he went back to the garden to watch the unicorn; but the unicorn had gone away. The man sat among the roses and went to sleep.

And as soon as the husband had gone out of the house, the wife got up and dressed as fast as she could. She was very excited and there was a gloat in her eye. She telephoned the police and she telephoned the psychiatrist; she told them to hurry to her house and bring a strait-jacket. When the police and the psychiatrist looked at her with great interest.「My husband,」she said,「saw a unicorn this morning.」The police looked at the psychiatrist and the psychiatrist looked at the police.「He told me it ate a lily,」she said. The psychiatrist looked at the police and the police looked at the psychiatrist.「He told me it had a golden horn in the middle of its forehead,」she said. At a solemn signal from the psychiatrist, the police leaped from their chairs and seized the wife. They had a hard time subduing her, for she put up a terrific struggle, but they finally subdued her. Just as they got her into the strait-jacket, the husband came back into the house.

「Did you tell your wife you saw a unicorn?」asked the police.「Of course not,」said the husband,「The unicorn is a mythical beast.」「That's all I wanted to know.」said the psychiatrist.「Take her away. I'm sorry, sir, but your wife is as crazy as a jay bird.」So they took her away, cursing and screaming, and shut her up in an institution. The husband lived happily ever after.

Moral: Don't count your boobies until they are hatched.

第 八 章 意群

你知道什麼是意群嗎？你知道下面的句子有幾個意群嗎？意群又是按什麼劃分的呢？

· Unless I visit every bookstore in town, I shall not know whether I can get what I want.

· We have two ears and only one tongue in order that we may hear more and speak less.

一、意群和語調群

從語音學的角度說，話語最小單位是單個的音素；從語音學和語義學結合的角度來說，最小的單位卻是語調群（Intonation Group）。語調群，是語言中語調的基本單位。一個語調單位通常相當於一個意群，由一個重讀音節和若干個非重讀音節組成。

在某種意義上，一個語調群或意群相當於中國現代詩歌裡的一個頓。例如：
輕輕的我走了，正如我輕輕的來。
要讀成：
輕輕的｜我｜走了，‖正如｜我｜輕輕的｜來。
不可讀成：
輕輕｜的我｜走了，‖正｜如我｜輕輕｜的｜來。

一個句子可以按照意義和語法結構分成幾個部分，每一個部分可稱為一個意群。意群通常是一個詞組或短語，當然也可以是一個詞或是一個句子。例如：

(1) ↗Really?
(2) ↘Certainly.
(3) 'Not at ↘all.
(4) 'All ↘right.
(5) I 'like it 'very ↘much.
(6) ↘Thank you, Sir.

一個語調群中最主要的是語調核心。一般說來，語調群中最后一個重讀音節上的下降或上升的音高變化就是語調核心，如上面第（3）句中↘all，第（4）句中↘right，第（6）句中的↘'Thank。如果一個語調群只有一個單詞，那麼這個單詞的重讀音節就是語調核心，如上面第（1）句中的↗Really 和第（2）句中

的↘Certainly。從結構上分析，一個語調群就是用重讀及音高變化的語音手段把一連串音素組合起來，並表達一定意義的語言單位。因此從「一定意義」這個角度來說，語調群又叫意群。意群在英語口語中起著非常重要的作用，能影響到說話者要表達的意思及情緒，在閱讀理解中也同樣起著重要作用。正確劃分意群能避免誤解甚至歧義，能更好地理解作者要表達的真正含義。

二、意群的劃分

正確劃分意群是準確表達的關鍵。意群是根據語義、語法和語調這三個因素來劃分的。從語義、語法上講，意群必須是能夠表達某種意思的一個詞、一個短語、一個從句、一個分句或一個獨立的句子；從語調上講，意群必須是可以用降調、升調和平調來朗讀的一個語調單位。意群與意群通常用符號「｜」分割。

(一) 依據語義來劃分意群

I'm busy.（一個句子即一個意群）

She told me｜she has changed her job.（兩個意群）

Yesterday｜he went to New York｜by air.（三個意群）

Before 1992，｜I used to live in Australia｜and worked as a doctor.（三個意群）

(二) 劃分意群的主要依據是句中詞與詞的語法關係

1. 偏正詞組（如冠詞與名詞、形容詞與名詞、副詞與動詞、名詞與名詞等）：an egg, bad boy, work hard, sun glasses。

2. 短語：in front of the car, to go home, sleeping dog, once upon a time。

3. 各種簡短的主謂句：

He looks pale.

We've given up.

He gave me a novel.

I heard you singing.

4. 各種簡短的從句：

What you say｜is not true.（主語從句）

The problem is｜who can get to replace her.（表語從句）

He made it quite clear｜that he preferred to study English.（賓語從句）

I have come here every month｜since I was a child.（狀語從句）

5. 如果句子很長，上述各種結構還可以按一定的規則劃分成若干意群。劃分長句的意群的原則如下：

(1) 用作主語的短語或從句可以有一個獨立意群，例如：

Many of the students｜like him very much.

What you say｜is not true.

（2）句首短語或從句用作狀語，可以有一個獨立意群，例如：

At that time, | he was very angry.

If you are tired, | you can have a rest.

（3）非限制性定語從句可以有一個獨立意群，例如：

This is his father, | who is a rich businessman.

限制性定語從句一般沒有一個獨立意群，例如：

He is the man I'm looking tor.

（4）非限制性同位語可以有一個獨立意群，例如：

I know his father, | a rich businessman.

（5）帶賓語從句的複合句，要在主句動詞和從句之間停頓，而不能在從句主語后停頓，例如：

（√）We hope | you have a good time at school.

（×）We hope you | have a good time at school.

（三）意群的劃分還同語速有關

同一個句子，語速快時劃分出來的意群可以少些；語速慢時劃分出來的意群可以多些。

Diligence | is the mother | of good fortune, and idleness | never brought a man to the goal | of any of his best wishes.

Diligence is the mother of good fortune, | and idleness never brought a man to the goal | of any of his best wishes.

練習

1. 朗讀下面的句子，注意意群的劃分。

（1）Once | two hunters went hunting | in the forest.

（2）One of them | suddenly fell down | by accident.

（3）He showed the whites of his eyes | and seemed to have ceased breathing.

（4）The other hunter | soon took out his mobile phone | to call the emergency center | for help.

（5）The operator said, |「First, | you should make sure | that he is already dead.」

（6）Then | the operator | heard a gunshot | from the other end of the phone | and next he heard the hunter asking, |「What should I do next?」

2. 給下列句子劃分意群，並說明理由，然后朗讀。

（1）They live in that large house on the other side of the bridge.

（2）Sometimes he was late, because his mother was in poor health.

（3）It is very important for us to take part in manual labour from time to time.

（4）Do you remember all those years when scientists argued that smoking would kill us but the doubters insisted that we didn't know for sure.

（5）However, whether it comes from the common ancestor that the species had 35 million years ago, is, as yet, an unanswered question.

（6）What is harder to establish is whether the productivity revolution that businessmen assume they are presiding over is for real.

3. 給下列繞口令劃分意群，並說明理由，然后朗讀。

（1）She sells sea shells on the seashore. The shells she sells are surely seashells.

（2）So if she sells shells on the seashore, I'm sure she sells seashore shells.

（3）I cannot bear to see a bear bear down upon a hare. When bare of hair he strips the hare, right there I cry,「For bear!」

（4）There once was a man who had a sister, his name was Mr. Fister. Mr. Fister's sister sold sea shells by the sea shore. Mr. Fister didn't sell sea shells; he sold silk sheets. Mr. Fister told his sister that he sold six silk sheets to six sheikhs. The sister of Mr. Fister said I sold six shells to six sheikhs too!

（5）How much wood would a woodchuck chuck if a woodchuck could chuck wood?

（6）A woodchuck would chuck all the wood a woodchuck could chuck if a woodchuck could chuck wood.

（7）How many cookies could a good cook cook? If a good cook could cook cookies, a good cook could cook as many cookies as a good cook who could cook cookies.

4. 朗讀下面這首詩，並注意意群的劃分。

What Is a Little Brother?

by Chris

What is a Little Brother? People ask.

It's someone that loves you more than enough.

It's someone that reassures you when life gets tough.

It's someone when you cry he cries to.

It's someone when you're feeling sad he comes up and hugs you.

It's someone that needs to feel protected.

It's someone of which murder you wish would never be affected.

It's someone that gives you a cute smile in the morning.
It's someone that gives you a frown as a form of warning.

Thankfully I've never had a frown as a form of warning.
I've always woke to a cute smile to start my morning.

A Little Brother is lots of things but the list is too tall.
But when a Little Brother dies he's the one thing you miss most of all.
(*http://www.poemslovers.corm/love_poems/family_poems/poems/2264.html*)

5. 朗讀下面的短文，注意意群的劃分。

Apology Helps

It is never easy to admit you are in the wrong. Being human, we all need to know the art of apologizing. Look back with honesty and think how often you have judged roughly, you said unkind things, and pushed yourself ahead at the expense of a friend. Then count the occasions when you indicated clearly and truly that you were sorry. A bit frightening, isn't it? It is frightening because some deep wisdom in us knows that when even a small wrong has been committed, some mysterious moral feeling is disturbed; and it stays out of balance until fault is acknowledged and regret expressed. A heartfelt apology can not only heal a damaged relationship but also make it stronger. If you can think of someone who deserves an apology from you, someone you have wronged, or judged too roughly, or just neglected, do something about it right now.

第九章 節奏

當一個句子中出現兩個以上的重音時，重音與重音之間無論有多少弱讀音節，它們相隔的時間基本相等，這種現象稱為「節奏」。

幾乎所有的語言都有節奏。語言的節奏與音樂的節奏十分相似。在音樂中，2/4 拍和 3/4 拍的節奏是「強、弱」和「強、弱、弱」。強拍（重音）都落在第一拍上。

樂曲簡譜如圖 9-1 所示：

2/4 拍樂曲

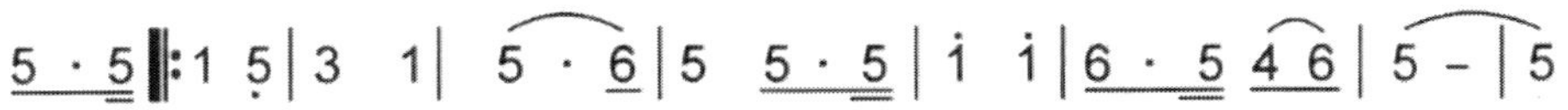

$$5 \cdot 5 \| : 1 \underline{5} | 3 \quad 1 | \widehat{6 \cdot 6} \underline{5} | \underline{5 \cdot 5} \underline{1} \underline{1} | \widehat{6 \cdot 5} \underline{4} \underline{6} | 5 - | 5$$

3/4 拍樂曲：

$$3 \quad - \quad 5 | \dot{2} \quad - \quad - | \dot{1} \quad - \quad 5 | 4 \quad - \quad - |$$

4/4 拍的節奏是「強、弱、次強、弱」：

$$\underline{3 \quad 4} | \underline{5 \quad 3} \quad \underline{1 \quad 5} | 6 \quad - \quad - \quad \underline{2 \quad 3} | 4 \quad \underline{5 \cdot 5} | 4 \cdot \underline{3} | 3 \quad - \quad - |$$

音樂的節奏一拍可以只有一個音符，也可以有幾個音符。例如：

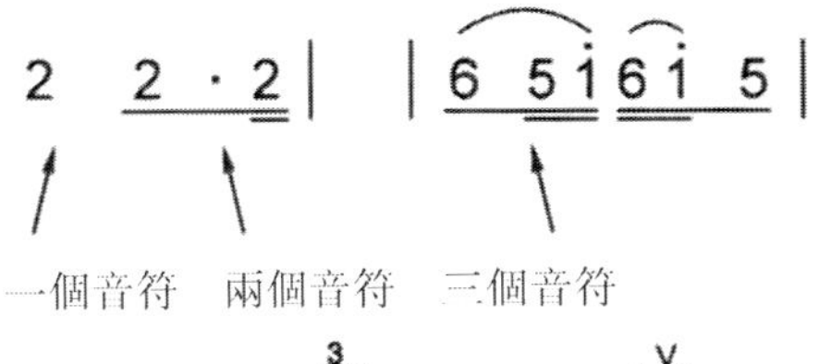

$$2 \quad \underline{2 \cdot 2} | \widehat{\underline{6 \quad 5} \underline{1} \underline{6} \underline{1} \underline{5}}$$

↑　　　↑　　　　↑
一個音符　兩個音符　三個音符

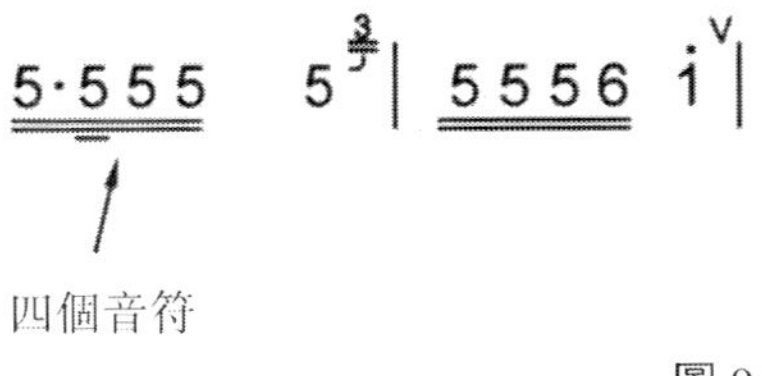

$$\underline{5 \cdot 5 \underline{5} \underline{5}} \quad 5 \overset{3}{} | \underline{5 \quad 5 \quad 5 \quad 6} \quad \overset{\vee}{\dot{1}}$$

↑
四個音符

圖 9-1　樂曲簡譜圖

與音樂一樣，英語的節奏由眾多重讀和弱讀的音節組成。本節所講的各種節奏模式用符號「O」和「o」的組合來表示。O 表示重讀音節，o 表示弱讀音節。當一句話只有一個音節時，這個音節只有一拍，一般重讀，但不構成節奏。例如：

Come! Go! Read! Thanks. Sure.

當一個句子是由兩個或兩個以上音節構成時，就有可能出現不同的節奏。例如：

Oo——Do it. Try it. Tell him. Practice! Sorry!

oO——Begin! Hello! He can. I do. I don't. Of Course.

當句子中出現兩個以上的重音時，節奏就變得比較明顯。兩個重讀音節之間的節奏是一拍。例如：

OO——Get out! No way! So what? Too fast!

OooO——Take him away. Do it again.

oOoooO 或 oOoOoo——I like him very much.

oOoooOooo——He didn't want to talk about it.

一個較長句子的節奏模式是由若干個較短的節奏模式構成的。這些較短的節奏模式一般可以按照意群劃分。例如：

I like him very much. 可以劃分為：

oOo/ooO 或 oOo/Ooo——I like him/very much.

節奏模式因說話者的意圖和感情而千變萬化。一句話可以有不同的模式組合。例如：

oOooOooooO 和 ooOooooOo——Ask 'not what your 'country can do for 'you, ask what 'you can do for your 'country.（John F. Kennedy）

或

ooOooooOoo 和 oOooOooOo——Ask not 'what your country can 'do for you, ask 'what you can 'do for your 'country.

句子越長，音節越多，其包含的節奏模式也就越多。但無論一句話中有多少模式，它的基本節奏是不變的。只要能夠正確地劃分意群，掌握好每一個意群的節奏，再長的句子，其節奏也不難掌握。

初練節奏的人應該注意以下幾個要點：

（1）一句話裡重音節太多或者太少都會喪失節奏。

'She 'came 'to 'see 'him.

（2）一個意群裡的弱讀音節原則上與其前面的重讀音節緊密連接，在前面沒有重讀音節時，應與后面的重讀音節連接。

She 'came to 'see him.

（3）兩個重音之間的弱讀音節越多，這些弱讀音節的讀速應該越快。

She 'came to 'see him.

She should 'come in order to 'meet him.

She should have 'come before it got so 'late.

正確掌握語言的節奏可以使意思表達得更加明確，而且使英語聽起來如同音樂一般優美、動聽、富有旋律。

練習

1. 常見節奏模式練習。

OO

Come here.	Try hard.	Work hard.
Stand up.	Not now.	Well done.
Sit down.	What for?	Why not?
Speak up.	Hold on.	So what?
No more.	Please do.	Stop that!

OoO

Write it down.	Try again.	Drive a car.
Have a try.	Not so fast.	Lend a hand.
What's it for?	Have a drink.	Go to sleep.
Move along.	What is that?	Break it up.
Do it now.	Practice hard.	Look and see.

oOo

I think so.	She's ready.	with pleasure
I'd like to.	I'm sorry.	as well as
Of course not.	Just listen.	at breakfast
I'd love to.	But why not?	without me
I have to.	I've read it.	at daytime
It's early.	She had to.	

oOoo

I think it is.	I've paid for it.
He wants us to.	a friend of mine
It's possible.	She came with us.
They've finished it.	Get rid of it.
I've heard of it.	It used to be.
He gave him some.	They knew it was.
It's beautiful.	He never was.
He said he would.	We forced him to.

OooO

Send him away.
What is the time?
Sing us a song.
Throw it away.
Where have they gone?
Where have you been?
Leave it alone.

Wait till I come.
Come for a chat.
No one is in.
Give him some food.
Show me the way.
What have you done?
Say it aloud.

oOoO

I think he can.
I want to know.
I'd love to help.
I think it is.
He thought he could.
He had to go.
It's all for you.

She took it off.
It's much too big.
It's very good.
It's hard to say.
a waste of time
a piece of bread
a cup of tea

oOooo

I gave it to her.
We had to do it.
I've written to him.
I've eaten them all.
I know what it is.
I asked if I could.

It's necessary.
We had to do it.
an exercise book
a quarter of it
in spite of it all
a long time ago

oOooO

I wanted to know.
I'll finish it now.
She asked me to go.
I thought he had gone.
He told me he would.
I've finished my lunch.

It started to rain.
It's clear he was wrong.
I'm sorry I'm late.
I'm glad you have come.
I'll see to it now.
We'll meet in the park.

OooO

Carry it away.

Hang it up to dry.

Put it on the desk.
Clean it with a brush.
Follow my advice.
Half of them have left.
How is Uncle John?

oOoooO
I hope it will be fine.
He wanted me to go.
There isn't any need.
I've heard of it before.
You're wanted on the phone.

oOoOo
I want to meet him.
I think you ought to.
I couldn't help it.
He never noticed.
You need a hair cut.
It doesn't matter.

oOooOoo
I'll borrow another one.
You'll get it on Saturday.
It's very unfortunate.
Perhaps you have heard of it.
It's not the right attitude.

OooooO
Show him up to his room.
Throw it into the fire.
Walking along the road.
Ready to go away.
Standing behind the door.

Put it on the shelf.
Let me take your bag.
Don't be such a fool.
Ask him what he wants.
Get him away now.

I waited half an hour.
It doesn't make much sense.
I didn't know the way.
So don't forget to come.
You mustn't do it.

You mustn't do it.
He left on Monday.
It's time for supper.
He hasn't got one.
She wrote a letter.
I'm not offended.

Let's open the other one.
The book isn't good enough.
He started to talk to me.
I don't want to frighten her.
We want him to come to us.

Why did you run away?
Tell him not to be late.
Ask them where they have been.
Fill it up to the top.
Finish it if you can.

第九章　節奏

143

oOoOoO

I think he wants to go.
It's not the one I want.
It isn't quite the same.
The train is very late.
I'm sorry I forgot.
There isn't time to change.

I hope you understand.
On Friday afternoon.
The concert starts at eight.
He goes to work on foot.
The roads are very dark.

oOoooOooo

It's not the one I borrowed from you.
He didn't think it interesting.
Remember what your teacher told you.
I took it to a watch repairer.
Perhaps you didn't quite realize it.
He didn't want to talk about it.
This isn't quite the moment for it.

oOooOooO

I'm looking for paper and string.
I think that he wants us to go.
I didn't expect to be asked.
She's gone for a walk in the park.
I've sent all the coats to be cleaned.
This envelope hasn't a stamp.
We don't want to trouble you now.
She'll never remember a thing.
Perhaps you can ring her tonight.

oOoooOoooO

We finished it the day before he came.
I wonder if he'll ask me in advance.
We haven't got an envelope to match.
The office-boy will show you where to go.
The factory is working day and night.
I didn't want to put him off again.
I don't suppose you'll understand my point.

The bus is more convenient than the tram.

2. 語速加快練習。

(1) We **bought** a **book**.

　　We have **bought** another **book**.

　　We could have **bought** you another **book**.

　　We ought to have **bought** ourselves another **book**.

(2) It was **good** to **speak** to him about it.

　　It would be **better** if you **spoke** to him about it.

　　It would have been **better** if you had **spoken** to him about it.

(3) He asked me to **give** him a **ticket**.

　　He should **ask** if we could **give** him a **ticket**.

　　He should **ask** us if we could **give** him another **ticket**.

　　He ought to have **asked** us if we could have **given** him a few of the **tickets**.

(4) He **cut** the **bread** with a **knife**.

　　He cut the loaf of **bread** with a blunt **knife**.

(5) **Tell** her to **put** it **down**.

　　Tell the girl to **put** the book **down**.

　　Tell the other girl to **put** the book on the **table**.

　　Tell the other girl to **put** all the books on the **table**.

第十章 語調

每一種語言都有其獨特的旋律。漢語的旋律主要表現為聲調，以字為單位，因而是聲調語言；而英語中的旋律主要表現為語調，以短語和句子為單位，是語調語言。

我們說話時可以隨意改變音高，使音調上揚或下降。音調的這種上揚或下降叫語調。語調是非語言交際的重要手段。不同的語調能使我們表達不同的情感，如：喜悅、悲傷、好奇、疑問、恐懼、驚奇、惱怒、憤恨等，從而傳遞出文字本身無法表達的微妙含義。沒有語調的英語就像一張白紙一樣沒有任何意義。語調的合理運用可以促進交際活動的正常展開，反之則可能對其產生妨礙。掌握並正確運用語調是實現有效交際的重要途徑，是英語語音學習的重要環節。因此，學習者應高度重視語調的學習。

一、英語語調

很多人都以為只要聽懂了每個英語單詞，就算聽明白了。但實際的情況是，只想著聽懂單詞，是遠遠不夠的。因為人們在說話的時候，往往伴隨著一些語調上的變化，這些不同的語調淋漓盡致地表現了人們懷疑、肯定、激動、感嘆等多種情感的變化。例如，你沒聽清楚別人的講話，希望對方再重複一下，就要說「升調」的 I beg your pardon.，但是如果你不小心踩到了別人的腳上，就要用到「降調」的 I beg your pardon.。看來同樣的一句話，由於「語調」的不同，意思也就有所差別。

我們說話時可以隨意改變音高，使音調上升或下降。我們還可以像歌唱家那樣突然抬高話語的音調。音調的這種上揚或下降叫語調。英語有兩種基本的語調：升調和降調。升降的過程可以是急促的，也可以是緩慢的，還可以形成不同的組合。說話人可以通過語調準確地表達各種信息。

英語語調或升、或降、或高、或低，一般都落在短語或句子的最后一個重音上，這和漢語大不一樣。為了便於學習和模仿，最終掌握英語的語調，我們大致將它歸納為以下四種。

  (1) 降調，在重讀音節中以 ↘ 來表示；
  (2) 升調，在重讀音節中以 ↗ 來表示；
  (3) 降升，在重讀音節中以 ↘↗ 來表示；
  (4) 平調，在重讀音節中以 → 來表示。

二、語調群

語調是語言的重要組成部分，語調通過與文字結合來達意。

語調的基本單位是語調群。通常一個句子為一個語調群，一個意群也可以是一個語調群，如前置的狀語或狀語從句等。一個語調群中至少有一個或一個以上的節奏群，每個節奏群中有一個重讀音節和若干個非重讀音節。劃分語調群的符號是「/」。例如：

/Hel·lo! /

/·Stand ·up. /

//For ·lunch/ ·Chinese ·people ·like ·rice and ·dishes. //

以上例句中，第一句有一個語調群，包括一個節奏群；第二句也有一個語調群，包括兩個節奏群；第三句前置狀語處運用了一個停頓，因而有兩個語調群，分別包括一個節奏群和五個節奏群。

三、語調核心

在一個語調群中，有一個音節特別響亮，並有音調的變化，這個音節就是語調核心。語調核心通常落在一個語調群的最后一個重讀音節上。例如：

/I ·don't ↘·like it. /

/·Nice to ↘·meet you. /

以上兩句均為由兩個節奏群組成的一個語調群。語調群末尾的最后一個重讀音節/laɪk/和/miːt/分別為該句的語調核心。

在語言實踐中，最常見的誤區是，許多英語學習者沒有語調核心的概念。當一個語調群應該讀成升調時，該語調群內的每個重讀音節都被錯誤地讀成升調，使得每一個重音都往上升，當然無法形成英語流暢舒緩的語流。

但是正如一句英語諺語所言「There is no rule without exception」，話語交際受講話人態度、情感和邏輯關係的影響，語調核心的位置也常常會發生轉移。例如：

—/·What have you been ↘·doing? /

—/I've been ↘·studying. /

—/Studying ↗·what? / /↗·Maths or ↘·English? /

—/↘·Neither. / /I'm ↘·sick of maths or English. / /I am studying ↘·Chinese. /

以上對話中「·」是重讀音節標示，「/」是語調群標示，「↘」和「↗」分別表示降調和升調，語調標志后緊隨的重讀音節是該語調群的語調核心。第四行/I'm ↘·sick of maths or English. /中，如果沒有上下文，語調群中最后一個重讀音節應該是↘·English，由於 maths or English 是上文已出現過的信息，不再是全句的焦點；sick 因為體現了講話人對問話人提出話題的強烈情感，反應了該句最突

出的矛盾，因而成為了語調核心。

再例如：

/I have 'never been↗'there，/but I↘'will 'go 'someday. /

此例后一語調群中 will 本不是重讀音節，更不是最后一個重讀音節，但是它的存在與前一語調群的含義形成鮮明對比，表達了強烈的主觀情感，因而成為了該語調群的語調核心。

四、語調的基本分類

英語中最常見的語調有三種：降調（↘），升調（↗）和降升調（↘↗）。

（一）降調的基本意義、朗讀和用法

降調表示「肯定」和「完結」，即講話人對所講內容肯定無疑，認為所表達的含義完整、語法結構獨立。例如：

Re'member to 'come 'back ↘'soon.

It's 'ni'ce of you to ↘'help me.

第一句 Re'member to 'come 'back↘'soon.中，句首的非重讀音節/ri/弱讀，起音很低，隨后出現的全句的第一個重讀音節/mem/音調最高，接下來的兩個非重讀音節/bə/和/tə/、兩個重讀音節/kʌm/和/bæk/音調依次緩慢下降，語調落在最后一個重讀音節，也就是全句的語調核心/suːn/上，音調明顯下降。

第二句 It's 'nice of you to↘'help me.中，句首的非重讀音節/its/弱讀，起音很低，隨后出現的全句的第一個重讀音節/naɪs/音調最高，接下來的三個非重讀音節/əv/、/juː/和/tə/音調依次緩慢下降，語調落在最后一個重讀音節，也就是全句的語調核心/help/上，音調明顯下降，其后的非重讀音節/mi/與之處於同一音調。

降調主要運用在下列句式之中：

（1）肯定或否定的陳述句用降調。因為無論含義是什麼，說話人對自己所表達的內容是沒有疑問的，含義和結構也是完整的。例如：

I'm glad to ↘meet you!

My home is very close to my ↘school.

I don't like speaking in a roundabout ↘way.

（2）祈使句表示強烈的命令或建議時用降調，強調內容毋庸置疑，聽話者毫無選擇餘地。例如：

Shut ↘up。

Don't ↘shout。

Keep off the ↘grass。

（3）特殊疑問句用降調，表示說話人濃厚的興趣。例如：

What shall we do ↘now?

Where are you ↘going?

How often do you read ↘newspapers?

（4）感嘆句用降調，表示感嘆。例如：

Oh, my ↘God!

What a ↘pity!

Look ↘out! ↘Danger!

（5）選擇疑問句的最后一個選擇項用降調，表示選項結束。例如：

Do most people like eating sweets or ↘meat?

How shall we go, on foot or by ↘bus?

Are you coming or ↘not?

（6）表達強烈陳述意味的一般疑問句或反義疑問句用降調，此類句子一般不需回答、言下之意明顯，與降調表達的「肯定」和「完結」相吻合。例如：

Are you ↘crazy?（表達出說話人毫無詢問的意願，主要是想提醒對方「你的舉動太瘋狂了」。）

Are you ↘satisfied?（表達出說話人毫無詢問的意願，並且非常確信對方會滿意現在的狀況，可以理解為「這下你應該滿足了吧」。）

You won't do it that way, ↘will you?（表達出說話人對於對方「不會那麼做」有很高的期待和信心。）

It's so cold, ↘isn't it?（表示說話人認為對方一定會有和自己一樣的看法。此句實際功能相當於朋友見面時的寒暄語，因為天氣是一個不涉及個人隱私的公共話題。）

（7）列舉多項事物時的最后一個選擇項用降調，表示列舉完畢。例如：

I like many kinds of fruits like water melon, apple, pear, strawberry and ↘litchi.

Students in the International College come from many different countries, such as America, Britain, France, German and ↘Argentina.

（8）置於從句之前的主句用降調，表示主要信息已結束。例如：

The boy was an↘noyed because his toy was badly destroyed.

The children ran away from the ↘orchard the moment they saw the guard.

Generally, air will be heavily pol↘luted where there are factories.

（9）帶非限制性定語從句、同位語或同位語從句的先行詞用降調。例如：

Yesterday I met ↘Tom, a friend of my brother's.

I heard the ↘news that our team had won.

He was quickly taken to ↘hospital, where a doctor wanted to examine his legs.

（二）升調的基本意義、朗讀和用法

升調多用來表示「不肯定」和「未完結」的意思，即講話人對所講內容不肯定，所表達的含義不完整或者語法結構不獨立。例如：

Has he come back ↗yet?

Will you do me a ↗favor?

如何正確朗讀以上兩句中的升調呢？

第一句 Has he 'come 'back↗ yet? 中，句首的兩個弱讀音節/həz/、/hi/起音很低，隨後出現的全句的第一個重讀音節/kʌm/音調最高，第二個重讀音節/bæk/音調稍稍下降，最後一個重讀音節/jet/為全句的語調核心，朗讀時從前一音節的音高位置開始往上讀成升調。

第二句 Will you 'do me a ↘'favor? 中，句首的兩個弱讀音節/wɪl/和/juː/起音很低，隨後出現的全句的第一個重讀音節/duː/音調最高，之后的兩個非重讀音節/mi/和/ə/音調稍稍下降，最後一個重讀單詞 favor 中的重讀音節/feɪ/為全句的語調核心，朗讀時從前一音節的音高位置開始往上讀成升調，非重讀音節/və/繼續呈上升趨勢。

升調主要運用在下列句式之中：

（1）一般疑問句用升調，表示疑問。例如：

May I ↗help you?

Would you like any des↗sert?

Shall I tell him to come and ↗see you?

（2）位於句首的狀語或狀語從句用升調，表示含義不完整。例如：

Time and time a↗gain I tried to hold back my sad feelings.

If you're not coming next↗week, I would travel alone.

To help my disabled↗aunt, I spend an hour working in her house every day.

（3）選擇疑問句的前半部用升調，表示含義不完整、結構不獨立。例如：

Shall we leave at↗six or seven?

Would you like a↗gin, or a↗whisky, or a beer?

Which vase shall I use, the short↗one or the tall one?

（4）反義疑問句的后半部，表示說話人有疑問，期待對方確認。例如：

I'm as tall as your sister, ↗aren't I?

You'd like to go with me, ↗wouldn't you?

Some plants never blown, ↗do they?

（5）列舉事物時，除最后一項以外的其他項用升調，用於區別語義。例如：

She bought↗red, ↗yellow and green rugs.

Chinese people are generally considered to have the virtues as↗hospitality, ↗industry and perseverance.

My daughter has a lot of toys: building↗blocks, water↗guns, toy↗cars, Teddy↗bears and Barbie dolls.

（6）一般句內停頓用升調，表示含義不完整、結構不獨立。「↗」為句內停

頓標示。例如：

By the↗way, /you're not expected to work here tomorrow.

Judging from his↗letter, /a campaign against「white↗pollution」/has been undertaken in his hometown.

China is making all her↗efforts/to strengthen scientific and technological cooperation with many countries.

（7）祈使句表示請求、道歉、關心、安慰等時用升調，使語氣稍顯柔和。例如：

Have a↗try.

I'm↗sorry.

Take it↗easy.

（8）問候、打招呼、提醒對方時用升調。例如：

↗Hi.

Take↗care.

Have a nice↗dream.

（9）偶有陳述句形式的疑問句，即陳述句後加「？」，應讀成升調，表示說話人對所表達的信息還有疑惑，期待得到對方證實。例如：

You↗like him?

He hasn't come↗back?

You'd like to go with↗Jack?

（三）降升調的基本意義、朗讀和用法

降升調是降調和升調功能的組合。通常是講話者對部分所講內容很肯定，用降調，但是又想表達一些言外之意，就轉為了升調。

降升調可以落在一個音節上，通常是語調核心。例如：

↘↗Yes.（部分肯定之前出現的信息，但還心存疑惑，希望還能得到更多解釋。）

↘↗How.（與降調不同的是，此句提問信息不完整，省略了許多信息，不能用單純的降調。由初始的降調轉為升調，突出了最重要的提問信息，並提醒聽話人去思考陳述句省略的內容，充滿回味。）

以上兩句均只有一個重讀音節/jes/和/haʊ/，均為語調核心，朗讀之初音調明顯下降，隨後以升調結束。

降升調也可以落在兩個音節上，降調標示重要信息，升調標示次要信息。例如：

He 'was↘very↗cute.（言下之意可能是「儘管這可能是他唯一的優點」。）

↘That wasn't very↗friendly.（言下之意可能是「儘管表面上看起來，這種行為很友好，但實際並非如此」。）

第十章 語調

151

以上兩句中，降升調均落在兩個單詞上。朗讀時應分成兩個部分，降調所在的單詞結束之前為第一部分，之後為第二部分。第一部分的朗讀方式參照一般的降調，第二部分的朗讀方式參照一般的升調。

降升調主要運用在下列情景之中：

（1）禮節性的寒暄或回應。例如：

—Mum, I got an「A」in the maths exam.

—Oh, ↘↗really?（Mum was in the kitchen.）

—You seemed not interested at all. Dad, I got an「A」in the maths exam.

—Oh, ↘↗were you?（Dad was watching a football game.）

（2）強調觀點的差異。

—I had an awful headache. Oh, I feel so bad that I will die.

—No, you ↘↗weren't.（強調頭疼是小問題，不會引起嚴重後果。）

（3）強調前後文對比時，前一部分用降升調比升調語氣更強烈。

I can find your ↘↗bag, but I can't find your key.

As to English, many Chinese students can ↘↗read, but can't speak.

（4）營造更輕鬆活潑的語氣時，如告別、祝願、鼓勵等。

↘See you ↗later.

A ↘good ↗job.

五、升降調的一般用法

（一）陳述句

1. 陳述句表示陳述一件事時用降調。例如：

I ↘understand.

It's ↘difficult.

Beijing is the capital of ↘China.

There is a book on the ↘desk.

They are going to have a ↘picnic.

The balloons are flying ↘away.

The birds are singing in the ↘trees.

Dennis is having a birthday ↘party.

2. 陳述句表示疑問時用升調。比較：

You ↘know. 你知道。

You ↗know? 你知道嗎？

He is a ↘doctor. 他是醫生。

He is a ↗doctor? 他是醫生嗎？

He has gone to ↘London. 他去倫敦了。

He has gone to ↗London? 他去倫敦了嗎？

3. 陳述句表示安慰、鼓勵和友好時用升調。例如：

A：This is the picture of my ↘wife.

B：Oh, she is ↗pretty.

A：My English is so ↘poor.

B：Don't ↗worry. I'll ↗help you with your ↗English.

4. 表示觀點有所保留、態度有所懷疑或猶豫，或有言外之意，下文有轉折（如but）時用降升調。例如：

A：Do you like the ↗house? 你喜歡這個房子嗎？

B：It's ↘↗new.（But it's small.） 挺新的。（但是小。）

A：Let's go to the theatre to ↘morrow. 咱們明天去看電影吧。

B：I can't go to ↘↗morrow.（But another day will do.）明天不行。（換一天可以。）

5. 用於糾正某人的話或表示相反意見時用降升調。例如：

A：She is a nurse. 她是護士。

B：A ↘↗nurse. 是醫生。

A：I can't finish the task. 我完不成這個任務。

B：You ↘↗can. 你能。

(二) 特殊疑問句及其答句

特殊疑問句一般用降調。例如：

↘Why? 'What ↘time is it?

When do you have ↘lunch?

'Where is the ↘factory?

但在下列情況中用升調。

1. 當提問過一次后，因沒聽清或沒聽懂對方的回答而又提問了一次問題時，用升調。例如：

A：When will you come ↘back? 你什麼時候回來？

B：In ↘January. 一月。

A：When will you come ↗back? 你什麼時候回來？

A：What's your ↘name? 你叫什麼名字？

B：My name is ↘Amy. 我叫埃米。

A：Did you say your name was ↗Amy? 你是說你叫埃米嗎？

2. 重複對方的問話以得到證實的疑問句用升調。例如：

A：When will the meeting be ↘gin? 會議什麼時候開？

B：When will the meeting be ↗gin? 會議什麼時候開？

（表示你是不是問會議什麼時候開始。）

153

3. 表示對所提問題很感興趣的特殊疑問句常用升調。例如：

A：I had a trip on the week↘end.　我週末旅行了。

B：Where did you↗go?　你去哪裡了？

A：I bought a ↘car.　我買了一輛車。

B：What's your car↗like?　你的車什麼樣？

4. 如果提問時表示溫和的態度用升調。例如：

How is your↗mother?

（三）一般疑問句

1. 一般用升調（答句一般用降調）。例如：

Is 'this a↗map?　'Yes, it↘is.

Is it↗Brown?

Do you 'often 'get↗letters from her?

Have you↗seen it?

Are you 'ready for the↗meeting?

2. 否定有時用降調（表示加強肯定的語氣，有時具有感嘆句的性質）。例如：

'Wasn't it a 'good↘film?

'Isn't it a 'fine↘day?　'Aren't they↘lovely?

3. 雖是一般疑問句，但在語句較嚴肅，或繼續提問時，或被要求重複這句話時，可用降調。例如：

A：Is↘this your um↘brella?

B：↗No, it↘isn't.

A：Is↘this it?

4. 表示懷疑時用降調。

↘Can she do it?

↘Will they come again?

↘Is it true?

（四）選擇疑問句

1. 在說話人所說的幾項中選擇時，前面的選項用升調，最后的一項用降調，中間的連接詞（如 or）用平調。例如：

Shall we↗walk or go by↘bike?

我們是走著去，還是騎自行車去？

Is your car↗blue, ↗green, or↘red?

你的車是藍色的、綠色的，還是紅色的？

Do you go there by↗bus or by↘taxi?

你坐公共汽車去，還是坐出租車去？
2. 如果說話人還有其他選擇沒有說出來，說話人說的幾項都用升調。例如：
Shall we ↗walk or go by ↗bike?
我們是走著去，還是騎自行車去？
Is your car ↗blue, ↗green, or ↗red?
你的車是藍色的、綠色的，還是紅色的？
Do you go there by ↗bus or by ↗taxi?
你坐公共汽車去，還是坐出租車去？

(五) 祈使句
1. 表示命令、語氣強硬的祈使句，句末用降調。例如：
Don't open the ↘door! 不許開門！
Don't make any mis↘takes! 別出差錯！
2. 表示鼓勵、態度親切或客氣的請求的祈使句，句末用升調。例如：
Don't worry about ↗that. 不要擔心。
Help your↗self, ↗please. 請自便。
Stand up, ↗please. 請起立。
3. 表示懇切的請求、責備或表示關心的急切警告時用降升調，第一個重讀音節用降調，句末用升調。例如：
↘Don't open the ↗door. 不要開門。（會冷的）
↘Don't eat so much ↗sugar. 不要吃那麼多糖。（糖對身體不好）
↘Put your coat ↗on. 把衣服穿上。（外面冷）

(六) 反義疑問句
反義疑問句前一部分用降調，后一部分有兩種情況。
1. 提問者對所提的問題沒有把握，希望對方回答時用升調。例如：
You will go to see ↘films, ↗won't you?
你是去看電影嗎？
They went to the ↘library, ↗didn't they?
他們是去圖書館嗎？
2. 提問者對所提的問題有很大把握，讓對方證即時用降調。例如：
He is from ↘China, ↘isn't he?
他是從中國來吧？
There are over one thousand people in the ↘hall, aren't there?
大廳裡有一千多人吧？

(七) 感嘆句
1. 感嘆句表示強烈感嘆時用降調。例如：

What a beautiful ↘car!

What a ↘nice day!

Oh, ↘dear!

How ↘nice it is!

2. 感嘆句表示驚奇時用升降調。例如：

A：I bought this dress for 500 dollars.

B：500↗↘dollars!

（八）狀語及狀語從句

1. 位於句首的狀語詞彙、短語或狀語從句一般用升調（有時用降調表示強調）。例如：

After↗supper, 'Grandpa 'Li 'told us about his 'miserable 'life in the ↘past.

↗Luckily, I passed the exam.

Last↗Saturday we 'worked in the ↘factory.

'When I was a 'little↗boy, I 'couldn't go to ↘school.

2. 位於陳述句句末的狀語從句一般用降調。例如：

He was↗absent because he was ↘ill.

We came↗home because it was ↘raining.

（九）並列句及並列謂語

並列部分一般前后均用降調。例如：

My 'family 'toiled for the 'landlord 'day and ↘night, but we had 'not e'nough food to↗eat or 'clothes to ↘wear.

He 'made the 'farmhands 'work 'long ↘hours but 'gave them 'little to ↘eat.

但如果兩個並列部分彼此聯繫很緊密（如具有「先后性」或「因果性」），那麼前一部分用升調，后一部分用降調。例如：

They 'knocked the 「thief」 ↗down and 'gave him a 'good ↘beating.

（十）列舉事物

除最后一個用降調外，其他一般都用升調，有時也可用降調，以示強調。例如：

They are↗Sunday, ↗Monday and ↘Saturday.

We have↗politics, Chi↗nese, mathe↗matics, ↗English and ↘other subjects.

（十一）插入語及引詞

1. 在句末時是作為語調尾處理的，它們延續句子主幹部分的語調。例如：

「My 'name is the 'P. L. '↘A. I 'live in ↘China,」 said Lei Feng.

「Both of you are 'really 'Chairman 'Mao's 'good ↘children,」 said all of them.

「Have you made up your ↗mind?」↗She asked.

He has 'gone ↘home, I think.

2. 如在句首，則根據意義的不同而使用升調或降調。例如：

Per↗haps, the meeting is ↘over.（Perhaps 用升調強調「偶然性」。）

↘Surely, I've told you that be↘fore.（Surely 用降調強調「肯定性」。）

By the ↘way, are you 'free ↗now?

3. 不在句首的插入語，有時也可自成一個語調組。例如：

It's like ↘this, you see.（或 ↗see）

↘↗Everybody, if it is ↗true, would ↘like it.（或… ↘true…）

（這句中的 true 用降調表示強調。）

練習

1. 標示出下列句子的語調群和語調核心。

（1）She's now in her thirties.

（2）Can you give me the book?

（3）Whom are you looking at?

（4）They won't forgive me.

（5）I will come to visit you tonight.

2. 給下列句子標上正確的語調，並朗讀出來。

（1）Will the meeting start at three or at four?

（2）He was unselfish, modest, and always putting the interests of others before his own.

（3）I'm not doing this for your sake.

（4）I'd love to go.（If only it were possible.）

（5）I don't think she was shy.（Whatever else she might be.）

（6）What will you expect?

（7）It's so unbelievable!

（8）You may do whatever you like, go wherever you choose and with whomever you please.

3. 朗讀並留意一般疑問句和答語的語調。

（1）Has he got a toy plane?

　　　Yes, he has.

　　　No, he hasn't.

（2）Am I going to have a birthday party?

Yes, you are.

No, you aren't.

(3) Is it really a dog?

Yes, it is.

No, it isn't.

4. 朗讀並留意特殊疑問句的語調。

(1) What do you want to eat?

(2) How much is a hamburger?

(3) When are we going to eat?

(4) Who can help me?

(5) Where is Simon's mum?

(6) How does Amy go to school?

(7) When and where was Helen Keller born?

5. 朗讀並留意選擇疑問句的語調。

(1) Could you come Monday, Tuesday, or Wednesday?

(2) Which country would you like to go to, England, Canada, or America?

6. 朗讀並留意反義疑問句的語調。

(1) David will have a birthday party, won't he?

(2) He is from Canada, isn't he?

(3) Lily will study abroad, won't she?

(4) She is from England, isn't she?

7. 朗讀並留意祈使句的語調。

(1) Don't take any chances!

(2) Stand up!

(3) Take off your coat!

(4) Close the window!

8. 朗讀並留意長句的語調。

(1) I like to go swimming during weekends or holidays.

(2) There is a book, two notebooks and a pen on the desk.

(3) After dinner I'll visit my uncle.

(4) Arriving at the station, we found the train gone.

（5）When I walked into the room, the telephone rang.

（6）He opened the door and Mary walked in.

（7）The left cup is yours and the right one is mine.

（8）We must start now or we'll be late.

（9）I'll go to America and Mary will go to Britain.

9. 說出下列對話中不同的語調表達的意思有什麼區別。

第一組

A：Mr. Smith thinks we ought to get the money in hand first.

B：↗Who?

A：Mr. Smith.

A：We'd like to have someone to say a word at the beginning to welcome the group.

B：↘Who?

A：We thought that you or Dr. Johnson might do it.

第二組

A：You will finish the work, ↘won't you?

B：Yes, I will.

A：You will finish the work, ↗won't you?

B：Yes, I will.（或 No, I won't.）

第三組

A：Are you Mr. Blake?

B：↘Yes.

A：Room Twenty-six.

A：Are you Mr. Blake?

B：↗Yes?

A：Ah, the secretary would like a word with you.

10. 朗讀下面的小故事，注意使用恰當的語調。

That Isn't Our Fault

Mr. and Mrs. Williams got married when he was twenty-three, and she was twenty.

Twenty-five years later, they had a big party, and a photographer came and took some photographs of them.

Then the photographer gave Mrs. Williams a card and said,「They'll be ready next Wednesday. You can get them from my studio.」

「No,」Mrs. Williams said,「please send them to us.」

The photographs arrived a week later, but Mrs. Williams was not happy when she saw them. She got into her car and drove to the photographer's studio. She went inside and said angrily,「You took some photographs of me and my husband last week, but I'm not going to pay for them.」

「Oh, why not?」the photographer asked.

「Because my husband looks like a monkey,」Mrs. Williams said.

「Well,」the photographer answered,「that isn't our fault. Why didn't you think of that before you married him?」

參考文獻

［1］BAKER, ANN. Ship or sheep? An intermediate pronunciation course［M］. Cambridge：Cambridge University Press, 1995.

［2］BEVERLY BEISBIER. Sounds great：intermediate pronunciation for speakers of English［M］. Boston, Mass.：Heinle & Heinle, 1995.

［3］Longman dictionary of contemporary English［Z］. 4th ed. UK：Longman, 2003.

［4］MACCARTHY, PETER. The teaching of pronunciation［M］. Cambridge：Cambridge University Press, 1989.

［5］JUDY B GILBERT. Clear speech［M］. Cambridge：Cambridge University Press, 1984.

［6］PAULETTE DALE. English pronunciation for international students［M］. Englewood Cliffs, N. J.：Prentice Hall Regents, 1994.

［7］ROACH P. English phonetics and phonology［M］. Cambridge：Cambridge University Press, 1994.

［8］ROACH P, HARTMAN J. English pronouncing dictionary［Z］. Shanghai：Shanghai Foreign Language Education Press, 1999.

［9］ROACH P. English phonetics and phonology：a practical course［M］. 2nd ed. Beijing：Beijing Foreign Language Teaching and Research Press, 2000.

［10］皮亞科瓦. 最新英語語音訓練大全［M］. 北京：北京語言大學出版社, 2009.

［11］葆青. 英語語音簡明教程［M］. 北京：外語教學與研究出版社, 1989.

［12］包智明. 生成音系學理論及其應用［M］. 北京：中國社會科學出版社, 1993.

［13］陳文達. 英語語調的結構與功能［M］. 北京：外語教學與研究出版社, 1990.

［14］方淑珍. 英語語音學基礎［M］. 廣州：廣東教育出版社, 1983.

［15］桂燦昆. 美國英語應用語音學［M］. 北京：外語教學與研究出版社, 1991.

［16］劉湧泉，趙世開. 英漢語言學詞彙［M］. 北京：中國社會科學出版社，1979.

［17］石鋒. 語音學探微［M］. 北京：外語教學與研究出版社，1992.

［18］許國璋. 許國璋英語［M］. 北京：外語教學與研究出版社，1992.

［19］張培基. 英語聲色詞與翻譯［M］. 北京：商務印書館，1990.

附　錄

附錄一　英語國際音標表

元音（20個）	長元音	/ɑː/　/ɔː/　/ɜː/　/iː/　/uː/
	短元音	/ʌ/　/ɒ/　/ə/　/ɪ/　/ʊ/　/e/　/æ/
	雙元音	/aɪ/　/eɪ/　/ɔɪ/　/ɪə/　/eə/　/ʊə/　/əʊ/　/aʊ/
半元音（2個）		/j/　/w/
輔音（26個）	清輔音	/p/　/t/　/k/　/f/　/θ/　/s/
	濁輔音	/b/　/d/　/g/　/v/　/ð/　/z/
	清輔音	/ʃ/　/h/　/ts/　/tʃ/　/tr/
	濁輔音	/ʒ/　/r/　/dz/　/dʒ/　/dr/
	鼻音	/m/　/n/　/ŋ/
	舌側音	/l/

附錄二　新舊英語國際音標對照表

元音	新	iː	ɪ	e	æ	ɜː	ə	ʌ	uː	ʊ	ɔː
	舊	iː	i	e	æ	əː	ə	ʌ	uː	u	ɔː
	新	ɒ	ɑː	eɪ	aɪ	ɔɪ	əʊ	aʊ	ɪə	eə	ʊə
	舊	ɔ	ɑː	ei	ai	ɔi	əu	au	iə	ɛə	əu
半元音	未變	j	w								
輔音	未變	p	b	t	d	k	g	f	v	s	z
		θ	ð	m	n	ŋ	l	r	h	ʃ	ʒ
		ts	dz	tʃ	dʒ	tr	dr				

國家圖書館出版品預行編目(CIP)資料

英語語音教程 / 許雪平、付博 主編. -- 第一版.
-- 臺北市：崧博出版：崧燁文化發行，2018.09

　面；　　公分

ISBN 978-957-735-487-7(平裝)

1. 英語 2. 語音

805.14　　　107015305

書　　名：英語語音教程
作　　者：許雪平、付博 主編
發行人：黃振庭
出版者：崧博出版事業有限公司
發行者：崧燁文化事業有限公司
E-mail：sonbookservice@gmail.com
粉絲頁　　　　　　網　址：
地　　址：台北市中正區重慶南路一段六十一號八樓815室
8F.-815, No.61, Sec. 1, Chongqing S. Rd., Zhongzheng Dist., Taipei City 100, Taiwan (R.O.C.)
電　　話：(02)2370-3310　傳　真：(02) 2370-3210
總經銷：紅螞蟻圖書有限公司
地　　址：台北市內湖區舊宗路二段 121 巷 19 號
電　　話：02-2795-3656　傳真：02-2795-4100　網址：
印　　刷：京峯彩色印刷有限公司（京峰數位）
　　本書版權為西南財經大學出版社所有授權崧博出版事業有限公司獨家發行電子書繁體字版。若有其他相關權利及授權需求請與本公司聯繫。

定價：300 元
發行日期：2018 年 9 月第一版
◎ 本書以POD印製發行